Vince

Lombardi

Paul Drewitt

Contents

Look on my Works, ye Mighty, and despair!

- Ozymandias

Chapter One

Sitting in that fucking boat pissed me off no end. I couldn't move, shit, piss, or do any of my other favourite activities. To make it worse, I sat next to this Russian wannabe-Iranian bloke. He was after political asylum, but I reckon he was a dealer. Not like these other peasants with nothing to their names except for a few well-spoken words like 'hey,' 'what,' and 'yeah.' They pissed me off every time I looked at them, bobbing up and down with the waves, thinking they're so fucking special, leaving a bad place and getting somewhere better. I was above 'em, mate, more sophisticated with smoother skin and perfect Wog English.

I was an Aussie once, living on the North Shore in Sydney. My last memory was leaving the airport, eating a Mars bar when the immigration guy was asking my name. I told the guy to fuck off and got detained for an hour, almost missing my flight. Dad was really pissed off and gave me a backhander when I got to my seat.

As soon as our asses touched on Muslim soil, Dad was jailed for posting a picture of the local Imam in a dress on Facebook, and I was forced to live with Grandma and my sixteen cousins. Our Aussie PR visas were cancelled, and that was that. I went fucking apeshit for three weeks. That was fifteen years ago.

'My name Karim,' said a stupid-looking fella sitting next to me.

'And, so what, cuz? You think I care. Fucking leave me alone,' I replied.

'We are brothers on the same boat.'

'Excuse me? Shut the fuck up, cuz. You're not my brother, okay? You're stupid anyway.'

'My name is Karim.'

I just left him sitting there with his hand outstretched.

'Okay, stand up, and I'll shake your hand?'

It was a sitting room only, one hundred and forty of us jammed in like sardines on our way to Australia from Indonesia. Everyone shuffled along as soon as someone got up, and you lost your seat. That was the plan.

'My name is Karim,' he said with his hand in my face.

'Get away, you dog. You're one of those Russian dudes, ay?'

'You want a friend? I offer.'

'Okay, I'll shake your hand, mate, but no promises. And I'll warn ya, people find me pretty fucking irresistible, mate, like a human magnet that never loses its power. Once you're in with me, it's like a spell, a really fucking strong one, mate.'

'Okay, shake. What name?'

'Vince, mate,' I said, shaking his hand. 'You a peasant like all the others?'

'I am proud Russian, hammer and sickle up your ass with broken glass.'

'Good one, mate, that's fucking good, ay. I like your shit talk, cuz.'

We smiled at each other, and that was that. I'd finally found someone to piss off no end.

By day forty-five, I'd managed to graduate to Chief Octopus Catcher. Me and Karim caught fifty a day and sold each leg for twenty-five cents. This kept the hoards satisfied and raised our social status to new heights. It sounds bad, I know, but living back in Lebanon was a whole lot worse. Those fucking prayer sirens and sharp rocky roads made me swear ten times a day.

To make it worse, I had to learn the language all over again without saying mate or cuz at the end of each sentence. It got so bad that in the end, the community banned me from the Church and burnt my prayer mat in the street. Octopus legs never tasted so good.

'Turn it over, cuz, more on the back, mate, keep going,' I said.

'You want cook? It's fucking octopus leg. Circle in shape – no back.'

I continued to rant with every Wog line in the book. No matter how much I gave the Russian, he never flinched. I never saw his hammer or sickle, not once. He was a true mate, someone I could lay shit on forever.

We ventured down below for what we hoped would be our last night at sea. We'd managed to build wall beds out of old sarongs the Iranian women didn't want, sixfold strong with real scout knots at each end. I slept bang on sea level with Karim just under me.

When I farted, he copped a direct hit and swore in Russian like a president drunk on vodka, cursing and waving at the invisible odor that went down on him hard and fast. It was hand-engineered humour in a dead-shit environment, where everyone either talked about the past or the future. Most wanted something good for their kids and not them or complained so fucking much about the way they'd been treated in detention centres. I admit, it wasn't a picnic in those places, but we were alive and kicking, so I told them to shut the fuck up every chance I could.

By sunlight, we could see the West Australian coastline. The boys in blue were used to Lebo boats coming in every week by that time, so my $12,000 investment was looking good. I managed to forge the insurance papers on my grandma's house, then burned it down just before I left Lebanon. The way I saw it, she owed me and Dad for something. Whatever that was, I'd think about later, but the fact was my arse was near freedom town, and I had myself to thank for it.

Me and Karim watched the coastline clear in the distance, waiting patiently for the speedboats to come out and meet us.

'Ay, where are you, ya dumb fucks?' I said, shouting out to the sea. 'Where's the fucking speed boats, cuz? You,

Captain, where are they, dickhead? Get on the phone and call em up, ya fucking brass-ass monkey.'

My charm had worked as he approached me with a metal bar. He was coming to help for sure.

'Boats,' said Karim.

'Finally. I'm getting on first.'

'Women and children, please to the front of the boat,' said the captain, still with a metal bar in his hand.

'C'mon, Captain, cuz, what's with the sympathy bullshit?'

I wasn't a wanker or anything. I just wanted to be first. Fuck the rest of them.

'We jump?' asked Karim.

I nodded.

'You swim in Lebanon?' he asked.

'Aw, shit yeah, mate. We dig wells out back, and we fall into 'em. Nice cool water three hundred metres down with a broken leg. Whaddya think? Take a nap, ya spastic!' I replied sarcastically.

'Then me?'

'What are you gonna say, mate?'

'Help.'

'Na, something better, cuz. Something clever, ya know?'

Karim looked back at me with a blank look. The one I saw on his face when I first met him that never went away. He was a dumb fuck, but I liked him.

'Okay, I'll do it,' I said. 'I'll just say I'm dying or something.'

When the boats arrived, I did a belly flop right in front of them. They killed the engine and spoke to me on a speakerphone, as if I was fucking deaf or something, cuz. Real fucking pieces of work, I'm telling ya.

'I can't swim, cuz. I'm dying…ya gotta save me, mate, c'mon,' I said, bobbing in and out of the water.

The head Aussie threw me a lifebuoy and told me to stay put.

Karim was laughing his fucking head off as they'd launched two ramps on either side of the boat. Turns out I was the last one to get on the speedboat and the only one to get wet. If I wasn't such a tough cunt I'd have been embarrassed or something, but living in a city with missiles passing over as I took a dump really hardened me up, ya know?

I walked on the boat and gave them the whole Scarface routine, saying that I was a political refugee and, 'I want it all, mate, everything that life has to offer, cuz. The world is mine. Welcome to my little friend and all that shit,' I even tried on the Pacino accent, but I quickly realised mine was better.

'Place the orange life jacket on and sit down on the front deck,' said the copper with the speakerphone.

He was talking to all of us, I think.

'Na, cuz, that's not me, mate. I'm not with them, ay, listen to the way I speak, ya dumb fuck. I'm Aussie, ay. I want special treatment,' I said.

'Sorry, sir, may I see your Australian passport?'

'What? I'm from the North Shore, so listen to how I speak, baldly.'

'I am Karim from Iran. Nice to meet you, good sir.

How are you?' said Karim from behind me.

Karim was keen to leave a good impression, or perhaps he was trying to save my ass. I had no passport, so I sat down and closed my mouth.

We sat on the front deck and watched them tie the boat.

'You are all being taken to the Perth Immigration Detention Centre, where your claims for refugee status will be processed,' said the bald guy with the speaker.

'When we are there, we stick together. Can be heated,' said Karim.

'Yeah, bullshit. You just want some of my mum's tabouli salad, mate.'

'You said North Shore live?'

'Yeah, mate, that's right. She'll be there to meet me, mate. You'll see. Now get your hand off my leg, ya try hard.'

I wasn't sure if I'd keep him around, as I had plenty of other friends on the boat. I reckon they were just too busy to talk to me, mate. It takes a lot out of the day to wash your clothes in seawater and not fall out of a boat.

Three other boats came out for a show when we finally arrived at the coastline. The paint jobs were new, and the crew looked like they'd just got out of high school. One of them picked up a speakerphone and dropped it into the water. What a fucking dickhead, cuz.

'Look at that one, cuz, he's got pimples,' I said.

'Vodka good for pimples, next kerosene,' replied Karim.

'You put kero on your pimples? What the fuck, cuz?'

I looked over his bumpy face and felt sorry for him. If he could do that as a teenager, then a detention centre would be gravy. Maybe I'd keep him around.

Karim and I chose the first bus in the line and sat up front. I could see the head dick was up front and wanted to get some leverage. He looked part-Wog, so I gave him the whole North Shore routine.

'Ay, cuz, how the fuck are ya? A decent citizen to finally latch onto, mate. I'm proud to be back, ay? Too fucking right, cuz.'

He said something in Iranian and pushed us into a

seat. No special treatment here, just a push-and-shove routine to keep order.

We arrived at the detention centre within ten minutes and were ushered into a courtyard. It had a fifteen-metre fence with demountable buildings scattered everywhere. It was like they built the fence first, then craned them over.

Our life changed when I saw Karim talking to a stiff at the fence line a few days later. He looked Middle Eastern and wore a nice suit, so I knew something was up. It didn't take long for the sneaky Russian to ask for help.

'I have a deal for you,' said Karim.

'And you need my help, cuz? What a surprise, mate.'

'You see fella over there?'

'Yeah.'

He pointed at an Iranian guy wearing tracksuit pants and Ugg boots. It could have been an Aussie.

'The government wants him gone.'

'That guy?' I said, pointing my finger.

'Call himself Arnie. The one who talk to himself.'

'Aw, yeah, cuz. So, what of it?'

'If we take care of the situation, the stiff at the fence can arrange a permanent visa, and we get out.'

'Just like that, cuz?'

'He says.'

I scratched my head a few times.

'So, you do it then?' I asked.

'No, you.'

'No, you, cuz. I'm the domesticated type. Can't you see?'

'So, all Russian are mobsters?'

'Pretty much.'

'Exactly. That's what all think. That's why you do it. He won't expect.'

And he was right. The sneaky Russian was even sneakier. He'd arranged a hit and knew I'd be the one to carry it out. But what could I do? Back home, the mobs pelted you with rocks or threw you down a deep well, head first. None of that shit here, so I needed to be creative.

I gripped the fence wire and stared onto the adjacent road. There had to be a way.

'I heard he has weak heart,' said Karim.

'So?'

'Plan around that. Maybe a midnight scare?'

'Good thinking, cuz, yeah. Do you think you can get hold of one of those speakerphones?'

'Dunno. Only in office building. Out of bounds.'

'Just say you're busting for a shit, cuz. Got the runs and can't make it back to the room.'

'You are crazy. You do it.'

'I'm doing the hit, cuz. You do it.'

Karim cracked his neck and roiled his shoulders back a few times, then ran towards the admin building with his hand on his arse, screaming and wailing that he needed a shit. The sneaky Russian pulled it off and dropped the speakerphone out the dunny window five minutes later. I was ready at ground level and quickly took it to my room.

The plan was simple: break into his room in the middle of the night and shout through the speakerphone five centimetres from his face. A heart attack would then follow, and the doctor's verdict would be 'death of natural causes.' We'd then have our visas, and the world is ours. Gone were the days of picking up rocks and nailing preachers to a cross. It was all fancy work, cuz. None of that crude shit of the past.

Karim woke me at 3 a.m., thinking that was the perfect time. The officials put the guy in a small demountable by himself, so we could do the deed without being seen or heard. Fucking lucky ay?

'Shut the fuck up, cuz. Can't you do that without the scratching noises?'

'Fucking Australian windows, mate. Always too tight,' replied Karim.

He continued to pry open the screen window. I could have brought a grinder and made less noise.

'There, get in,' said Karim.

It was pitch-fucking-black in there. It took a few minutes for my eyes to adjust.

'Over there, get him.'

Suddenly, a light turned on in the corner. He was sitting at the kitchen table, eating peanuts.

'Want me? Huh? Always, they come and go. Now I show you,' he said.

We packed shit and held hands. It was like an involuntary reaction.

'You stinky dogs. I … I …' He began to cough. Slowly at first, then fell onto his hands and knees.

'Hit him.'

'With what, cuz?'

'Speakerphone.'

We were still holding hands.

The Iranian collapsed onto his stomach and lay there, dead still. We moved over to the table where he was.

'He's choked, cuz.'

'No shit. Unsalted peanuts, look,' said Karim, holding the bag in the air.

I searched for a pulse on his neck, but I probably looked in the wrong spot. Anyway, he looked dead, and we weren't asking for help. It wasn't murder, just a type of manslaughter or borderline Murphy's Law. Whatever happened and how it happened was fate in all its beauty.

Karim gave the signal at the fence the next morning, and we got our visa interviews the same afternoon. I felt like Tony Montana all the way, cuz. Take it to the limit, reach the point of no return, and take it further. I even did the *'say hello to my little friend'* thing to all the other detainees. They were impressed, and they just didn't say it to my face.

'Lombardi! Vince Lombardi, come forward,' said a fat white guy in the admin building.

I walked in and sat down.

He had a badge and stripes on his shoulders, so I knew he was somebody. It was time to lay it on thick, wog-style.

'Hey, how are ya, cuz? You're a big man, cuz, eh? Two of me easy.'

He just sat there with a poker face. He had everything in front of him ready to stamp, but he was going to make me sweat.

'You 'Jimmy's' really makes me laugh. Do you think you can just walk in and make yourself at home? And don't think I don't know how that fella died.'

'I swear to God, cuz. I'm innocent.'

'Horseshit! I was watching you dickheads from the observation tower. I was the one who gave him the peanuts. Don't you think I want a promotion too? Don't you think I want to get the fuck out of here and into the Perth head office?'

'Ah, I dunno, cuz. Can you stamp me, mate?' I said, looking at the paperwork.

He was starting to get evil on that chair. Karim and I had sleazed him out of his promotion. It looked as if the Iranian government had placed an open hit on the guy, and we just happened to cash in. Life was looking up, cuz.

Just after midday, we were standing next to an Ampol service station with our paperwork. Not a dime to our name and nowhere to go. The pricks dropped us off like we'd just been kidnapped or something. They didn't even talk to us, keeping to themselves in their own little world, talking about how hot the new intern was or how to get divorced and still live under the same roof. If you wanted to get divorced in Lebanon, you got both feet cut off and had to wheel around on a homemade cart, fending off the wild dogs with a stone in each hand. These Aussies had it easy cuz.

'I have a mother here,' said Karim.

'Where? Here? She works at the Ampol, cuz?'

'Idiot, she's eighty-five. Somewhere in Fremantle.'

I knew there had to be a reason why a Russian needed to pose as an Iranian. Family can be a strong motivator.

'So can we knock her up for a bed and some spare cash?'

He didn't respond.

'What's your last name, cuz?'

I'd never thought to ask in the last forty-five days.

'Ivanov.'

'Great name, cuz. Can you say it with a smile?'

'What?'

'I mean, can you say anything with a fucking smile?'

I was trying to get some emotion out of him.

'Shut up, wog boy. If we can find, maybe we get money.'

'Okay, let's ask the Ampol guy.'

We walked into the service station and lined up with

everyone who was buying petrol. There was a chick behind the counter with tats covering both arms, constantly chewing on gum like a moo cow on heat.

'Oh, hey, cuz. Me and Karim just made our way here by boat and managed to get out of the local centre. Can you help us out, cuz?'

'I'm calling the police,' she replied, reaching for the phone.

'Aw, shit, cuz, it's the absolute truth, cuz, you gotta believe me, cuz, ay? We just need some help.'

'With what?' she replied, taking her hand off the phone.

'We're looking for an Ivanov lady, around eighty-five, who has money.'

'What the fuck? Here's a phone book.'

She threw a two-inch book our way.

We sat out on the curb and found three Ivanovs in Fremantle.

'Hey, lady cuz, thanks for the help, ay,' I said on my return.

'Put it on the counter and fuck off!'

I liked her attitude. She reminded me of my big sis back home on the North Shore. I hadn't seen her or Mum for fifteen years, or any of my other two hundred and seventy-five cousins.

We waited across the road for a bus that never came. The Ampol chick must have thought we were stalking her. Just when we thought of walking it, she came out with her handbag and hopped into a beat-up Datsun 180 B.

'Get in,' she said, jamming on the brakes in front of us.

'What for?' I asked.

'I'll take you to Fremantle, no further.'

I hopped in the front seat, and she gave me a *fuck me* stare. I'd heard of chicks like her; the one's that abuse the living shit out of ya when it's really a come-get-me technique. I was all over it, cuz. Karim just sat in the back, trying to imitate my style.

'I like your arms, cuz – all ink and no hair. It really turns me on, cuz, ya know? Can I turn on the radio? Where's the on button, babe? Can I put my hand on your leg?'

Her grip on the steering wheel tightened.

'I've got a brother like you,' she replied.

'You a wog girl? I knew it, cuz.'

'No, you idiot. He's disabled, too.'

I knew there was a reason she wasn't making fun of me. I'd misread the signs.

'Aw, wow, hey?'

Karim began to laugh in the back seat. One of those sneaky fucking Russian laughs start in the gut and doesn't get any further.

'It's okay, I'll help you out. What's the first address?' she asked.

I wanted to get out there and then. My first tag-on with an Aussie chick resulted in a disabled claim. I was fucking devastated, cuz.

We arrived in Fremantle five minutes later and got off midway on High Street. I played the whole sympathy thing and gave her a kiss on the lips and ran my hand along her back. It was the first trim I'd had for God knows how fucking long. Tasted good and felt even better.

We stood there looking at the traffic, pondering our next move. Karim worked out that all the odd houses were on one side of the road. He was impressed.

'Number two-three-one, unit twenty,' said Karim. 'Down this way, on the left.'

We walked side by side, watching everyone go about their business. It was our first encounter with society for some time. Everyone had a sense of purpose that was a pure habit – people shopping, going to work, and socialising. No one seemed to have anything to win or lose. They just existed, knowing what they were doing without even having to think. We'd made the big time.

'So, is she alive?' I asked Karim.

'Mum?'

'Yeah, that's the one, cuz.'

'Was the last time I saw her.'

'When?'

'Russia. A long time ago. I got info from the KGB for ten bottles of Vodka. Good deal.'

Karim produced an old crinkled printout from his back pocket. For a price, you could waltz into the local Moscow office and buy whatever information was on the computer. If you didn't have money, cigarettes, or booze, then a quick pleasure session behind closed doors was of equal value. There was always a way to pay.

I took the paper and tried to read whatever I could.

'This is twelve years old, cuz.'

'All I have. You have something better?'

'Yeah, in Sydney.'

'We in Perth.'

I sighed and told him to lead the way.

We arrived at a block of apartments at the end of High Street. It had old shops all around with shit everywhere.

'Number twenty,' said Karim.

'No number twenty … only goes up to ten.'

'Check again.'

'Don't need to, mate. The letter boxes right in front of us.'

I paused.

'You wanna go to Sydney?' I asked.

'Big smoke?'

'Yeah, with me. I've got family there.'

'Big?'

'Massive, mate. The last count was 275.'

'275? You the king of bullshit, or what?'

'Nice one, cuz. You're learning from the best mate. Stick with me; I'll show you the world and teach you proper English. Shit, I'll even let you kiss me when we get there.'

He thought for a bit, then screwed up his paperwork. He threw it onto the ground with an effortless underarm action, like he didn't have any energy left at the moment. I could tell he was hell sad, ay, so I didn't lay on the typical wog bullshit. I had manners when it counted.

'So, you came all this way to see your mum?' I asked.

'Yes and no.'

'What's the no part?'

'Russia cold. Tell you what to do, when to wake up, people watching on the corner ...'

'Okay, mate, I get it.'

From that moment on, we were hitched, like friends with something deep in common. More than just the usual cool stuff. We were orphans in a foreign land.

'Okay, let's walk,' said Karim.

'Where?'

'Sydney.'

'Na, mate, we bus it. It's four thousand kilometres. Greyhound is over there. I'll swing us some tickets.'

We strolled over to the local terminal and sat in the waiting room, looking for a sympathy vote. The head lady asked if we needed some help, but we didn't respond. We needed a miracle.

'You two again. What are you doing?' asked a girl from behind us.

It was the Ampol girl with tattoos on her arms.

'Veronica, it's you,' screamed Karim.

'What are you doing here? Russian, where's your

mum?'

'My name Karim.'

'Karim, where's your mum? You better not have been bullshitting me?' she said in a mamma wog tone.

'She is not there. Building long gone. See,' said Karim, pointing his finger.

Veronica stood there with her arms folded.

'So, you need more help?' she asked.

We nodded.

'Jesus Christ, can't you lot help yourselves? I'm not a charity benefit.'

'Then why did you ask, mate?'

My logic hit hard. I reckon she liked me, cuz. I was in for sure.

'We're going to Sydney,' I said.

'With me?' she replied.

'I guess so, if that's where you're going.'

'We happy family. What a country,' said Karim.

'You got any money?' She said with her arms crossed.

'Not a penny, mate,' I replied.

She looked at me again with that brother-lookalike sympathy. I was milking it to the max.

Within two hours, we were on the bus to Sydney, sitting in the back row with our shoes off. Veronica sat in the middle, listening to music, acting like we weren't even there. She threw in a pie with sauce and an iced coffee at the servo, so we were right for food. The only thing left to do was sleep.

After the thousand-kilometre mark, we'd got all her backstory. Veronica lived in Sydney and was travelling around for a break. She warmed to us pretty well, as she hated snobs with cash. It was like being home again with me cousins, reading a Lebo fairy tale with my jammies on.

She asked us tons of questions along the way. Her fingers ran up and down her arms every time she asked me something private like she was nervous that I'd get pissed off. Most of the questions were directed at me, as I could spin a good wog yarn. Karim just answered in short, pithy sentences, which needed no real response.

By the two-thousand-kilometre mark, our minds

were turning inside out. There was fuck all to look at, and pretty much every bush looked the same. The road seemed to go on forever, like a never-ending one-way street.

'Jesus fuck Christ when we get there? Take me back to Russia,' said Karim.

'Let's rob the next service station?' I asked Veronica.

'Great idea, boat boy.'

At least it was an idea.

'So, you haven't told me. What's the plan for Sydney?' she asked. 'You going to call Mum and help her cook lunch five days a week like a good little boy?'

'Not me, cuz. Me and Karim got plans, babe.'

'Oh, yes, that's right. The world is yours, ay? Take it to the limit?'

Karim smiled with a cigar in his mouth that he'd found on the ground.

Chapter Two

By the time the sneaky Russian had come out of the chemist, there were cops everywhere. Getting a criminal record for stealing a pair of tweezers just didn't seem worth it, so we ran for our lives and met up with Veronica at KFC.

'What the fuck have you two been up to?' she asked.

'Aw, nothing, ay cuz. We were looking for you, ay Karim?'

'What the hell is he doing?'

'Aw, not sure, ay. Karim, what's up mate?'

He sat there cross-legged on the floor, pulling out his nose hair.

'Get off the floor, ya dumb fuck. Do I need to pour Vodka on your head or something? Use a chair, cuz, like a normal person.'

We began to draw a crowd.

'That's it, I'm not hanging around with you drop kicks any longer. I'm finding you a job, and that's it.'

'What? No happy ending with me and you getting the

same tattoo and screwing on the beach? I'm really fucking disappointed, love, I'm telling ya.'

'Will you just shut the fuck up and listen?'

I heard a cheer from behind me. Must have been about something else.

'Now, I know a coffee van in King's Cross. The fella is looking for two drones to make basic stuff like Barista coffee and sandwiches. Can you handle that?'

'Barista fucking what? Sounds pretty exotic, babe. Does it have booze in it or something?'

'No, it's a type of coffee.'

Karim laughed.

'Shut up, Vodka boy. Did you know what it was?'

'Hey?'

'See, there you go. Just sit there a pull your extra thick nose hair.'

'Why are you so mean to him?'

'Because he can't speak properly. Problem?'

Veronica puffed up her cheeks and stared at me.

'Ok, so what's this van with Barista booze and something called a sandwich?'

'It's in King's Cross.'

'Aw yeah, you told me that.'

'Yeah? So do you want the job or not?'

'Let Karim decide.'

She looked down and saw him chewing on a nose hair.

'How about you decide?'

'What's the guy's name?'

'Does it matter?'

'Not really, I just wanna know.'

'It's a job! Do you want it or not?'

'Ok, let's meet the guy. But if he's not cool and sophisticated like me, I'm blowing him off quick smart.'

'Yeah, you do that. And you can use his nose hair for the clean-up,' she said, pointing to Karim.

I didn't get her humour.

Two hours later, we were standing in front of the most hideous fat fuck in the history of all fat fuckers. The guy was fucking huge, as big as anything I'd ever laid shit on.

'Vince, this is Billy.'

'Huh?'

'Billy, this is the guy I was talking to you about.'

I stood there staring at him, moving my eyes up and down his body, which had obviously been tortured with lard, saturated fats, and MSG.

'You're a big fuck, cuz?'

'Hey?' he replied.

"I mean, you're fat. Biggest fat cunt I've ever seen.'

Billy looked around like I was talking to someone else.

'You talking to me?' he asked.

'Yeah, mate. It's a nice way to break the ice. Say it like it is, ya know? None of that tinker bell shit at my end. Not my style, ay?'

'You don't like fat people?'

'Aw, yeah. I mean, no, well, it depends.'

'On what?'

'Lots of stuff, mate. Why, what's it to ya?'

The guy held his hands in the air and said something in Slovakian.

'We want a job. Work hard and have no complaints. Please try. I like Slovakia, great sausage. Not too much salt,' said Karim from behind me.

'Speak for yourself, cuz. I want superannuation, free food and drink, a massage from a hot chick every half hour, and unemployment insurance in case I get fired in the first ten minutes. Are you listening to me, fat boy?'

'Yeah.'

'Well, good. If not, clean your fucking ears out, cuz.'

'You guys are really something,' said Veronica.

'Ok, it's ok. They can be a comedy team. I like it, yeah, I get it. You staged all this to impress me. You guys are really smart, eh?' said Billy.

Ten minutes later, he was showing me how to use the Barista machine. I had to wear this fucking apron that said 'welcome to the fun house' and tie my hair back in a ponytail.

'You see these buttons?'

'Oh na, mate, I'm fucking blind.'

He laughed and smacked me on the ass.

'These are different types of coffee. You understand?'

'Doesn't all coffee taste the same?'

'Coffee is good. I like it cold,' said Karim, standing in the background.

No one replied.

'Isn't coffee just coffee?' I asked.

'There are many types. Just ask what the customer wants, make the coffee, and take their money. Got it?'

'Aw yeah, cuz, no worries. What do you want Karim to do?'

'You, Russian, wipe down the bench.'

'That's fucking it? Why am I up front?' I asked.

'You are most funny. Nothing funny about a Russian who never smiles. Not good for business.'

Five minutes later, a classy Australian girl came up and smiled at me.

'How the fuck are ya, love? Are you a wog girl?' I asked.

'Sorry?'

'Aw na ay, you look too prim and proper. You must be from somewhere else.'

'Um, sorry, can I have a short black please?'

I leant over and gestured for her to come closer.

'It's a fucking scam love.'

'Scam?'

'Yeah, you've been living it your whole fucking coffee life, ay.'

She was a little taken aback.

'It's all the fucking same, babe. Coffee is fucking coffee.'

She stared at me and broke out laughing.

'What is this? Where's the camera? Did my boyfriend make you do this?'

'Aw yeah, cuz, is he that fat cunt standing over there?'

Her smile turned upside down.

'Short black, please!'

'Na, I can't do it to ya love. I'll just press all the buttons and move the cup underneath. You'll love it, trust me.'

'Will it taste like a short black?'

'Just stand there and fucking wait. Don't talk to me again until I'm finished.'

I pressed every button on the machine and ran the cup underneath while Karim entertained the young lady.

'You like Vodka?'

'Vodka?'

'Yeah, clear white booze with kick to guts.'

'I know what Vodka is.'

'You want come back to my place?'

'And where is that?'

He began to stutter.

'Fucking leave her alone, you sneaky Russian. I'm making her a coffee.'

'Do you like me, babe?' asked Karim.

'Um, well, you're very different.'

'You just feeling sorry for the prick, love. Trust me, he's not you're type. Look, he's got dried Octopus legs in his front pocket, see!'

I put my hand in his pocket and felt a flawless, well-sized Willy Hammond.

'You touched my dick!'

We enjoyed an uncomfortable silence.

'Is my coffee ready?' she asked.

'Here, drink that.'

She took a few sips.

'Tastes like all the different types in one cup.'

'You like it?'

'Not really,' she said, giggling away.

'Hey, what are you up to today?'

'Fuck wog, I saw first!' yelled Karim.

'She doesn't like you, mate. I'm more sophisticated.'

'Actually, I've got a boyfriend. Do I need to pay for this?'

'Aw yeah, that'll be $46.80.'

'Why?'

'Because you had all the coffees in one cup.'

She handed over a $50 note, which I placed in my pocket.

'So anyway, what are you doing today?'

'I'm going walking in the mountains.'

'Aw yeah, my cousin in Lebanon did that for years. One day, he got lost in the middle of summer and had to drink his own piss. Have you ever done that?'

She turned and walked away.

'Jesus, ladyboy. You suck,' said Karim.

'What the fuck, cuz? I almost had her, ay? Was it the piss comment?'

'You two get out here,' screamed Billy from the back of the cart. We piled out the back and stood tall in front of Fat Billy boy.

'I've had complaints about swearing, not giving customers what they want, and asking people if they drink their own piss. You're supposed to be funny, not offend people.'

Karim turned away and walked over to a parked car.

'Hey, Russian, this is for you too, ya know?'

'I reckon we've had enough, mate.'

'You've been here for thirty minutes,' said Billy.

'Yeah, well, that's me top to bottom, cuz. I've got potential coming out of me asshole mate. I'm surprised I lasted this long with my IQ and charm, ya know?'

'Right, fuck off, the two of you. You're fired! And I'm telling Veronica about all this.'

Ten minutes later, we were talking to some weirdo and his mate in a parked car.

'This is Buster. He put a hit out on the Iranian guy at centre.'

'The one at the fence?'

'Na Eshay brah, that's an agent. I'm totally up the food chain, brah ay. I work for the man himself,' said Buster.

'Brah?' I replied.

'Yeah, Brah, it's pig Latin. You understand me, ay?'

'So, you're a pig?'

He got out of the car dressed in Adidas track pants, Nike shoes, and a sports cap.

'You starting something, Brah? You want a piece of me, Brah? You need to Illchay ay Brah, just cool down ya gronk.'

'Ok cuz, all good cuz ay. Let's just all cool down, cuz, brothers. We're all on the same boat.'

'Ok Brah, that's eetswa Brah, ay?'

Buster got back into the car and began to talk with Karim.

'We've got a staunch coming up, Brah? You up for

it?'

'Staunch?' asked Karim.

'Yeah, a job, sting, deal, ya know?'

'What work?' asked Karim.

'Chum fuk wa,' cried a voice from the passenger seat.

'Oh yeah, Brah, this is Limmy. He's with me,' said Buster.

'No good bak ta. This is one staple to fak ya pool table. Mincemeat chum tucker!'

'Aw no, cuz ay, not the fucking Triads. Karim, what the fuck is this mate?'

'Easy, Brah, all good, ay. He's just muscle, that's all.'

'Gik wap nok chop suey.'

'He says that he doesn't like you, Brah.'

'How about you, cuz?'

Buster rubbed his chin for a bit.

'Dunno, Brah. I was going to offer you a street deal

situation, but you two look like something way special. A couple of stand-up super Brahs, ay?'

Sounded kinda kinky.

'Na brassa, kim look duffy. Kill.'

'Hang on, Limmy, let's give em a chance to pull off a major gonk, Brah.'

'Hells Angels imp bik gonky tuffer.'

Buster poked his head out the window and looked us over.

'Can you handle a machine gun, Brah?'

'You talking to me, cuz?'

'Both of you.'

'I work for the KGB in Russia. We kill anything, with anything, whenever asked.'

'You never told me that, cuz.'

'Because you never talk to me.'

Wow, it was like I was getting to know a whole new Karim. Secret agent for the KGB and all. Really fucking impressive, I'm telling ya.

'Brah, a KGB on the staff. Wait until I tell the boss.'

'Still fak chum tucker pool table.'

'He said he wants to nail you to a pool table and chop you up, and if you fuck this up, I'll let him have his way ay adlays? You two Brah's better do well.'

Limmy started to pick his teeth with a meat clever.

'Do well what?' asked Karim.

'Kak no info.'

'Aw yeah, sorry, Brah. The Hell's Angels are coming into town from Newcastle. They say they've got three kilos. If you go there and bring it back, you got three grand adlays. You keen?'

'Three kilos of what, cuz?'

'Kak snort bubble bath.'

'Aw yeah. That stuff. Gotcha cuz.'

'Here's the address, Brah. Tomorrow afternoon at 5 p.m. Here's the ashcay buy money.' Buster handed over an envelope.

'And if anything happens to that ashcay Brah, ow

you adlays ay!'

'Chum tucker pool table wog boy. Kim rip balls!'

Karim smiled, totally unfazed by what'd been said. I wondered if he understood.

One hour later, we were still in the same position, analyzing a street map we'd ripped from a phone book.

'What fuck, upside down?'

'Yellow pages cuz, always fuck everything up ay. Ripped off cuz.'

'You did the rip.'

'It was fucking necessary, alright. Who needs a phone book when you make a call these days?'

'Hey, you two, back to work,' screamed Billy from the coffee trailer.

'Hey, look, coffee fat dude, we've met Limmy and his adlay with the ashcay, and we're stalking some angels for three kilos. So, we don't need you're toxic fucking coffee anymore. Anyway, one cup costs $50. You're going bankrupt, mate, in a massive downward spiral to hell.'

Billy waved us on and made a call on his mobile

phone. I knew he was talking to Veronica, so I gave Karim a look and crossed the street.

'So, where the fuck are we?'

'From here?' asked Karim.

'Ay?'

'From there to here.'

'Are you trying to tell me we're lost, cuz?'

Karim studied the yellow pages map singing the Russian national anthem.

'Ok fuck it! We sleep in a homeless shelter and catch a taxi to our deal tomorrow. Plan?' I asked.

'The world is mine?'

'Yeah, if you like. Hey, that's my line! Sneaky fucking Russian.'

The next day, we piled out of a homeless shelter and washed our faces at a fountain on Macleary Street. It was pretty fucking impressive with a centerpiece that looked like a snowflake. The water tasted like a spew.

We sat at a pie floater cart for two hours feeding the pigeons, who seemed to enjoy anything we threw at them. I couldn't work out why someone would eat a pie swimming in pea and ham soup, mate.

'Why didn't you order something else, Russian? What the fuck is this?' I asked.

'Pie floater. He says tradition from Adelaide.'

'This is Sydney, mate. Never fucking heard of it.'

'He says.'

I looked at the menu and saw twenty variations of a pie floater, motivating me to take on the Hell's Angels and improve my life.

'Eat up, Russian. Tomorrow, we'll be eating at a restaurant. High and mighty cuz with dames by our side ready to put out at a moment's notice, mate.'

'Put what out?'

'Never mind, cuz. I guess that's one more trick I need to teach you, ay?'

'Women?'

'Yeah, women, cuz. You need to know how to handle them, like that babe at the coffee trailer yesterday.'

'Aw yeah, when you told to drink own piss?'

'That was fucking different! I was looking out for her cuz. And it's true, mate. Most people who get lost in the wilderness need to drink their own piss. I was just trying to help.'

'So, you need to tell her?'

'Yeah, she'll be back for it, cuz, you wait and see. Just like that Veronica girl. She likes me, ay?'

'I think her name is Verbonica?'

This Russian was spoiling every cozy moment I was trying to create.

'So, what plan for 5 p.m.?' asked Karim.

'We pick up the 3 kg from the bikers and meet back at the coffee van.'

'Then?'

'Then, whatever happens, mate. It's life calling us to whatever and whoever. Can't you feel the excitement in your blood, Russian?'

'Yeah.'

'Are you sure? You don't look any different.'

'I'm excited!'

I moved over and looked into his eyes.

'I can't tell.'

Karim had a look that never changed from one moment to the next. He was a stone-cold mother fucker that could lie his ass off, then tell the truth with the very same look. He helped me to understand my thoughts, as everything I said to him bounced back or was met with a disturbed reaction. He was either a hard core dump fuck or just naturally subdued.

Between him, me, and us, we were going places. Right to the top of the world, sipping cocktails and peeling bikinis on a sandy beach. I dreamt of the day I could eat Baklava served on a well-toned Victoria's Secret ass, talk shit with a real movie star, and slag off a dense politician to fit in with the crowd, mate. The Angel's deal would secure all this and more.

At 5 p.m., we were standing outside a Best Western motel with our fists clenched and a mouthful of saliva.

'The Angels are tough dudes, cuz. Are you ready?'

'For what?'

'For tough stuff, mate.'

He looked at me again with that 'I don't know what the fuck you're saying' look. If anything, the guy was reliable.

'You know, gangster shit cuz, ya know?'

'Na.'

'Look, we go in with the ashcay…'

'Huh?'

'The money, the fucking money!'

'Yeah.'

'Then we buy the 3kg and take it back to Buster.'

'3kgs?'

'Yeah, the 3kgs!'

'Of what?'

'Bubble bath, mate. That's what Limmy said.'

'Who?'

'The Chinese guy who looked like a chopstick. The bloke with the Eshay.'

'Yeah, it makes sense. How much money is in your wallet?' he asked.

'You mean buy money?'

'Hmmm.'

I opened it up and counted fifteen thousand smackers.

'We run with loot?' asked Karim.

I thought hard and long, and it must've been at least ten seconds.

'Na cuz, we need this deal to work our way up the chain. I want the world, mate; fifteen grand is only the start. We need to go in.'

'I'm getting way, driver.'

'Yeah, that's really smart, ay? A getaway driver with no fucking car. Whatta you gonna do, piggyback me down the road?'

'What that?'

'Ow fuck it, we go in and do what men do. We take on the world and come out strong, mate. You follow?'

'Who in there?'

'Buster said two fully patched Angels selling bubble bath. Must be the really fucking expensive shit, ay? Let's go.'

We walked single file to room 62, looking over our shoulders all the way. When we arrived, a bloke resembling Captain Caveman opened the door and asked us for ID.

'What is this? Jesus H Christ, God damn fucking foreign shit. Can't buster send a true-blue swinging dick to the man's house? You got the money?' he asked in a thick Texas accent.

'You're American, cuz.'

'Too fucking right. Born in the heart of the very clean and United States of USA. I'm so fucking American I stink of apple pie, and when I wipe my ass, there's never any mess. You follow?'

'Jesus mate, you've got more personality than me.'

'Well, if I actually knew you, then I could comment on that one, couldn't I? Who's the stiff next to you?'

'My name is Karim.'

'Russian?'

'Hmmm'

'A fucking communist?'

'No, that's my dad.'

'Oh, so you admit it, your dad sent you to spy on me. Is that right?'

He was saying all this shit from the doorway.

'Look, cuz, Buster just sent us to collect the bubble bath. Then we're gone.'

The American burst out laughing.

'Oh, my fucking lord Jesus Christ. I've never heard it called that before. You're a fully-fledged swinging dick, my man. I like ya. The name's Riso.'

By this time, a crowd had gathered behind us. I just hoped there were no cops among them.

'Vince, Vince Lombardi.'

'You're last name's Lombardi? You got to be fucking kidding me? Dolores, get the fuck out here and meet this new swinging dick that's arrived at our porch. He's something I'll tell ya.'

An older-looking chick came out and stuck her head

under his arm.

'Well, Whatta ya think?' asked Riso.

'Can he cook? He looks like he can,' said the chick.

'Look, mate, cuz and cuzina, we're just here for the bubble bath. Ok?'

They looked at each other and handed over a package. It was wrapped up in an American flag.

'You bring this all the way from America?' I asked.

'No, what makes you think that? Are you trying to stereotype me? You God damn self-righteous slimy goat fucking son of a bitch?'

'You like music?' asked Karim.

Riso slammed the door, pissing himself laughing, then opened it again ten seconds later and took the money. When I turned around, there were twenty or so people staring at me.

'Aw, it's just bubble bath, ay. I swear to God cuz ay, you gotta believe me.'

Karim grabbed me by the arm and led me into a waiting taxi.

'Jackpot Vodka! You clever mate.'

'Did you hear that guy cuz, fuck me ay? The guy put me to shame. I wish I could talk like that.'

'He's clever. He like music, eh?'

'Yeah, I guess so,' I replied, looking out the window.

'Show me the bubble bath.'

I unravelled the American flag and saw three packages of white powder.'

The next day, we sat next to the coffee van disguised as refugees. I wore a Sarong around my head, and Karim rubbed dirt on his cheeks. Billy took a few looks in our direction, but he was flat chat ripping off the community.

We saw Buster drive by a few times but were too ashamed to flag him down. After a few pass-byes, he stopped to check us out.

'Eshay Brah! You adlays do well?' asked Buster, pulling the handbrake. 'Yeah, cuz the American dude was all over it, ay? We got the bubble bath.'

Limmy and Buster looked at each other and laughed.

'Yeah, Brah, the bubble bath. You adlays ay? Crack

me up.'

'Sho like fun boys.'

'Too right, Limmy ay. Now pass over the stuff.'

Limmy spent a few minutes weighing it on a fancy scale.

'Jim fuck mom, fifteen kilos,' said Limmy with his hands outstretched.

'You sure, Brah?'

'Honey king prawn.'

'Riso gave you this?' asked Buster.

'In doorway shouting,' replied Karim.

'Soup head USA. Boss, back seat said Limmy.'

'You think so, Brah, these two?'

I stood there with a Sarong on my head, waiting for payment.

'This is good for you two, ay Brah. Fifteen kilos instead of three. Boss gonna be pleased with you two adlays ay?'

'Gim back seat. Chim chopper!'

We piled into the back and buckled up.

'You're privileged young ladies. Don't usually do this, but ay Brah, you're gonna be in the good books. This is how ya work, ya way up ay Limmy?'

'Chook tucker shark shit. Best practice.'

'Too right, Brah.'

We travelled for an hour into the heart of the city and went into an underground carpark.

'Out chum lover,' said Limmy.

He made us stand to attention at the back of the car.

'Now, Brahs. You're about to meet the head dick. His name's Tex.'

'Sounds common,' replied Karim.

'It's from the bible, Brah. You got a problem with that?'

Karim shook his head.

'Low profile or rip and strip. Love ya dick?' asked Limmy.

'Yeah, cuz ay. Full respect.'

'Some bock ya, Dad,' replied Limmy, two inches from my face.

The place was like a Lebbo palace mate, with marble pillars and shiny tiles all over the fucking place. We walked around in circles for a bit, slamming into the pillars that seemed to be more of an obstacle than an attraction.

'Boss, brah, I've bought the bubble bath,' said Buster.

'Tim fak boss, me Limmy.'

'Where is he, Brah?'

'Fak know.'

Suddenly, a familiar voice echoed from a balcony.

'You fucking Lilly livered sons of bitches. You're nothing but badger shagging, corn pone, trailer camp, preacher porn loving, half-baked white fucking trash.'

'Boss, ease down, Brah. That's not good for morale, man. You hear?'

'Don't you fucking patronize me ya tracksuit pant Nike wearing varmint. You're nothing but a hound dog, and a sticky one too. Get up here, all of ya, and bring your chopstick loving brunette shag ass boy with ya. Now hurry up, you hear?'

Jesus, fuck me, cuz. This guy had more personality than an overgrown Chimpanzee with a university education.

It took three fucking minutes to climb the stairs. When we finally arrived, we collapsed with exhaustion.

'Get up, you sons of bitches. I ain't paying you to sleep on my badass shag carpet, am I? Hang on, who are you two?'

'I think we've met cuz. We bought the bubble bath today?'

'Bub, what?'

'The shit wrapped in a flag, cuz. It was only three hours ago.'

Limmy and the brah boy looked puzzled.

'Ay, so think all Americans talk the same way. You hanging apple on me, son?'

Limmy took out the bubble bath, wrapped in an American flag.

'Fifteen kilo, boss, pay for three.'

Tex scratched his head with apple pie under his

fingernails.

'So, you brought this back? Jesus H Christ, there are still some honest people in this world.'

He shook his head and looked at the ground.

'I'm impressed. You made me proud. I feel like you're my own children standing in a house of God. Like an Amish preacher getting teary-eyed because he doesn't know any better. Hail to the chief, ooh, that red, white, and blue!'

'Wow, cuz, so you're religious? Like me, cuz, with my prayer mat and blazing sirens fifty times a day. We're gonna get along fine.'

'Jim hold tongue, gip suck?'

'Now hold it down, Limmy. The boy has a mind of his own, and I respect that. Let's see how this all pans out.'

'Whatcha gonna do, Tex, brah? You're up 12 kilos ay?'

'It's not the bubble, Brah laddy, it's the trust factor.'

'Aw yeah, Brah, I get it, ay?' he said, looking confused.

Tex looked long and hard at me, then averted his

gaze to Karim.

'Russian, you KGB?'

'How to know?'

'I don't, you fucking idiot, that's why I asked.'

'I kill anything, with anything, however, whoever with whatever.'

'His specialty is unsalted peanuts, cuz.'

'Stick in the throat? Jesus fucking fat-free smallgoods, unsalted peanuts, uh? If that doesn't take the cake on the fourth of July. You're a smart mother fucker Russian, even though you look like a turtle with little or no ambition.'

'No, like boss, pool table nail time!'

Tex looked over to the pool table and shook his head.

'Na, I don't think so. These guys have the potential to make things happen. Between all the Vodka shots and the Allah screaming going on, they'll make us fucking millionaires. Suit them up and show 'em the ropes.'

'Hang boss?'

'No, you stupid meat clever Peking duck marinade, I meant show em the business inside and out. You, Brah boy, you speak English?'

'Inside and out, Brah, ashcay and all ay? On it, Brah boss lad.'

'Alright, come in and have a drink. I've got apple pies in the oven and French fries converted to American chips. Business is finished, let's party.'

He took us into a large room with three different coloured sofas and a bar in the corner. I sat on the red sofa and watched the others choose between white and blue.

'Whatta ya have Russian?'

'Vodka.'

'What a fucking surprise. Did I even need to ask?'

'Ask what?'

Tex poured eight shots and gave them all to Karim.

'That's so I don't have to talk to you again. How about you, Vinnie boy?'

'Prune juice, chilled.'

'Say again?'

'It's Wharf's favourite drink on Star Trek.'

'Oh, I see, the violent Monkey on TV who never smiles?'

'That's it cuz, he's my hero ay?'

'Well fuck me sideways, you're gonna bring some skills to this family, aren't you?'

'Ay? Family?'

'God damn right! You're part of a holistic star-spangled banner unit of preacher porn love fun, my boy. We all stick together here. You ok with that?'

'Yeah, cuz,' I replied with teary eyes.

'Why you crying boy? Did I say something to upset your internal spastic insides?'

'Na mate, I just thought of me, Mum, cuz. She's here on the north shore somewhere.'

'Well, we can help you with that as well.'

'Haven't seen her for fifteen years, ay cuz. Won't even know what she looks like.'

'Eshay brah, she dresses in black, cooks five times daily, and has piano legs. Am I getting warm, brah?'

Karim laughed whilst Limmy shaved his chest with a meat clever.

We drank and swore into the afternoon, watching reruns of the 1987 Super Bowl final between Atlantic City and Utah. Tex screamed 'yi-ha' every time leather touched skin and drowned himself in Kentucky straight bourbon whiskey, whilst everyone else covered their ears and swore in a foreign language. My only respite from the bullshit was piss breaks on request, and on number fifty-seven, I heard the front door slam.

'Honey, I'm home,' screamed yet another familiar voice.

I walked onto the balcony and saw a good-looking babe enter an elevator. Did she get out of climbing the stairs just because she was good-looking? Fucking hot dames.

When the doors opened, I saw Veronica all dolled up in makeup and designer clothes.

'Vince? What are you doing here?'

'Aw shit, it's the lady cuz that's made it big overnight? Too hoo, Ampol babe to bubble bath babe in a heartbeat ay?'

'What the fuck are you talking about? Where's the

Russian?'

'Who Karim?'

'You know any others?'

'Ah, he's inside eating apple pie. Are you married to that yank inside?'

She paused and looked over my shoulder.

'Sophia, you too good for me little darling chick ling? Come over and give Uncle Sam a slushy tongue wobble for old times' sake,' said Tex.

'Jesus' fuck! You know this star-spangled cock?' I asked.

'Watch your goddamn mouth, you underage son of a middle-aged bitch.'

'Ease down on him love, he's with me,' said Veronica.

'With you? You mean you've been searing this guy's T-bone steak?'

'Na just travelled on a bus with him, and he's ok. Give him a break.'

'I've been breaking the bitch since I saw him. Even

got him dealing in the bubble bath. Did a fine job too. I was about to welcome the slut into my twin tower family.'

'You mean that Arab plane job a few years back?' I asked.

'No, you dumb shit, this house has two towers. Like my two fingers, see?'

He gave me the V for the Vendetta signal and started to pash with Veronica. I wondered why my efforts at feline trim were knocked back in Perth.

One hour later, I was standing in the same place watching tongues woggle.

'So where to from here, Veronica, cuz? Can you help us out again? I don't wanna go home to Mum a failure, ay. I need to show her I'm a success at something. It's about pride, babe.'

Veronica took her *Jaba the Hun* like tongue out of the American's mouth and shook her head.

'You fucked up that coffee van job right and proper. Fat cunt told me you were lecturing people on what to buy, saying that all coffee tastes the same.'

'It does, babe, it was my honest and full-blood wog

answer. I was helping 'em, mate.'

Tex interrupted.

'Well, I'll tell you what I'll do. I know just about every swinging dick in this town. If you can't find a career after I've finished with you, then it's back to bubble bath dealing on the streets with Buster and his lowlife.'

'Eshay, boss badass. We do other stuff, ay Limmy?'

'Fuk duck until red.'

'Yeah, Brah, you do a mean red duck at the corner takeaway! Adlay all the way brah!'

Buster took out his steak knife and rubbed it on Limmy's meat cleaver. It made a seriously mad sound, cuz.

'Ok, so Buster, send these two new immigrants around the traps. Stop by Pablo's house first and see if he needs a hand. I'll be at the party later today and want to be entertained. You streaks of pelican shit need to step up, you hear?' asked Tex.

'Step up is good with army shoes on,' replied Karim.

We watched Veronica nodding all the while, and I wanted to stick it to her, but I wanted to impress Mum more, so we four boys skipped down the stairs and out the front door. As I looked back, Veronica was on her knees fixing Tex's belt, or that's what it looked like from my angle, ay?

Chapter Three

We drove around for an hour listening to Buster's rap music. He kept on zipping and unzipping his tracksuit top to annoy us, and Limmy had his head between his knees, curling his pubic hair round his little finger.

'Are we going to Pablo's cuz?' I asked.

'Too right, Adlay. Gonna clown up for the boss's old mate son.'

'Clown up?'

'The entertainment industry, Wog boy. Right up your pizza alley, ay?'

'Extra fuk buk cheese.'

Everyone was laughing except for me. I wondered if Karim understood.

'Ay, cuzzers, shouldn't we just stick with the bubble bath? It's pretty straight forward: just rock up with cash and hand over the flag. Good business.'

'You got to work your way up the chain, Brah! Anyway, you said you wanted a career adlay; you want to go home to your Mum and say *I wake up each morning and buy packages wrapped in a flag with a fully grown lad and his chopstick sidekick?'*

I shook my head.

'Well, the entertainment industry is there for you adlay, so hang tight, we're almost there.'

We eventually parked around 100 meters from Tex's twin tower joint, cuz. When Buster killed the engine, a half-dressed South American came out of the front door and stared us down. Limmy waved his meat cleaver out the window and ushered him over.

'Clown cok these two. Tex dig ya?'

'Eshay Pablo, it's you adlay. You look fucked up ay?'

'Cok suk pig manner.'

'Eh gringos, you came to help the man with the clown suit. We gonna make a big show today, you lovers,' said Pablo with a smile. 'We got honey bears coming to the big birthday party, and Tex doesn't wanna be sad about it.'

We piled in the front door expecting to see a hoard of party cuz boys and their personal cooks, but the fucking place was empty ay cuz. Not a lady in black anywhere, or a hanging red duck, nor a pair of tracksuit pants. Our boy, Tex, must have decent friends, like white boys in suits who rip everyone off down the pecking order and make laws in Canberra just to feel useful. I felt privileged just to be there.

'Get in the room gringos, and take your fucking clothes off,' yelled Pablo.

I was hesitant, but Karim looked excited. He began to make hooting sounds and wiggled his shoulders up and down.

'This is business, vodka boy. We're now in the entertainment industry,' I said.

'How?' asked Karim.

Pablo put his head over my shoulder.

'You're gonna dress as clowns and entertain the kids. Once the makeup is on, no one will know you're foreigners.'

'Ain't you a foreigner, cuz?'

'No, because I eat meat pies and pretend that I like AFL, that makes me Aussie. Now, get in there and get dressed. My wife will help you with the makeup.'

One hour later, we emerged looking more like monsters than clowns. Our makeup was watery, and our outfits were way too fucking small. Karim kept winging that his balls hurt, and my yellow wig smelt like a clean-up rag for a geriatric wanking contest. I couldn't fucking breathe cuz, I'm telling ya.

'Ok gringos, everyone's out back ready to go. Come out after I've introduced you and work the crowd. Remember, woo the kids as it's a birthday party.'

'Fucking hang on, we don't have any experience. How exactly do we 'woo' mate?'

'You just flap your arms about and smile.'

'Fuck,' replied Karim.

After Pablo left, I had a few shots of whiskey from the booze cabinet to get warmed up. Karim skulled a whole bottle of Vodka and almost chucked on the carpet. We drank so much that we had to eat something.

'Pantry, lots of flour,' said Karim.

'Yeah, so, you gonna make bread?'

But I was too late. He was so pissed that he poured half a packet of self-raising flour down his gob. He then ate a whole tub of butter and a jar of olives from the fridge. Buster and Limmy were looking through the window at us, pissing themselves laughing, pointing at the guests arriving in droves, all dolled up in pink dresses, stardust hair, and ruby-red shoes.

'Gringos, you're on,' yelled Pablo from out back.

The first ten minutes were smooth sailing, as we were right in character. The jolly clowns that laughed and waved their hands about, mate. But it all turned sour when Karim chucked in grandma's lap whilst she was eating birthday cake. It was the chuck from hell, a concoction of Vodka, butter, flour, and olives. Really gave the lady a fright. Pretty soon after, the parents started to pull their kids from the party, running onto the road, dry reaching all the way.

One minute it was standing room only, then it was just us bubble bath crew, with Tex and Veronica standing at the back, looking a little worried. To make things worse, Limmy had tied up the cat, making death gestures with his meat cleaver.

'Hold the fucking civil war!' screamed Tex from the back fence. He'd been standing there with Veronica as an onlooker, trying not to cause a scene. 'Jesus, fuck my endangered critter. You really know how to fuck up the unfuckable, don't ya? Jesus H Christ, all you needed to do was dress up and laugh with the children.'

'But maybe they need training?' said Veronica in their defense.

'Yeah, I agree ay cuz. We just got nervous ay, that's why all the drinking and stuff. It was all nerves, I reckon, ay Karim?'

By that time our Russian boy was out cold, lying on the grass with his tailor-made chuck all over him. We decided to leave him out of all further discussions for the time being.

'Pablo, whatta you think about this situation? Shall I order Limmy to get his clever stained for honour and glory?' asked Tex.

'Hmmm…maybe not. Perhaps Veronica is right, you know? Maybe the gringos need training. What about a stint at the carnival down the west side? A couple of days, and they'll be side-show alley material, no?'

Pablo was the manager of the Patch Club, a carnival on the outskirts of town with clowns, rides, shooting games, and all the bullshit that goes with it.

'Let's give the gringos another chance,' said Pablo.

'Well, tickle my hairy brown asshole. You people make me cry more than Jimmy Hendrix with an American flag wrapped around his fully erect bad boy. I'm touched, I really fucking am.'

'I'm all for more training. They've got potential,' said Veronica.

'Yeah, I guess, apart from drinking in front of children, eating flour, and vomiting on the elderly, yeah, I can see your goddamn point, babe.'

Tex always had a way of putting things, like he was the supreme lord of one nation that saw the world as his very own basketball, rotating in his palm. The kind and lonely lord of the universe that sat at the head of the United Nations and never said a fucking word, knowing only too well that the deal was already done behind closed doors.

After a few dick rubs from Veronica, Tex agreed to let me and Karim work at the Patch for a few days. I reckon it was all due to those sensual fingers rubbing up and down his pants. But I still reckon she liked me, as she was looking my way all the time cuz. I remember the day we met in her beat-up Datsun 180B, when I stroked her legs as she accused me of being disabled. It was all just a cover-up cuz, a really fucking good excuse not to jump me right there and then because Karim was in the back seat.

So, it was all organized, mate, we'd get all the training we needed from Pablo at his carnival of fun, then I'd be an entertainer and make Mum proud. There wasn't a day that went by that I didn't think of Mum and my 275 cousins, waiting for me on the north shore. I tried to send a letter to her after I burnt down my Aunties house to claim the insurance money for the boat ride to Australia, but I felt kinda guilty for all the shit I caused, so I chucked it down a well just before I arrived at the post office in Lebanon.

We arrived at the carnival car park at 5pm. Karim was still passed out in the back seat with his head on Limmy's lap. He was slowly shaving his head with his meat clever.

'Dim vodka hair,' said Limmy.

He was tasting his hair, mate, one strand at a time, like some kinda fucking cannibal.

'I need to take a shit Gringo,' said Pablo.

'Yeah, ok, cuz, what are ya telling me for? It's your

fucking carnival, mate.'

'Yeah, yeah, I know Gringo, but I'm just letting you know I might be a while.'

'You all choked up, cuz?'

'Na, it's just that now I'm a little older, the clean-up gets harder. You know what I mean, ay Gringo?'

'Eshay, brah, what the fuck?'

'Fok dim no register.'

Karim was snoring.

'Look, Gringos, when you get a little older, like me, it takes longer to wipe up the goods. Gets messy, you know?'

'What the fuck are you on about cuz? Just spit it out in your well-mannered, fucked up South American accent.'

'Ok, every time I take a shit, I need to take a shower afterward.'

'You can't wipe your ass properly, cuz?'

'No, no gringo, it's not that.'

'Then why do you need to take a shower, mate?'

There was a long silence.

'Ok, ok Gringo, you got me. I can't wipe so well. Are you happy?'

'Very fucking happy cuz, I'm gonna tease the living fuck outa you.'

By this time, Karim was sitting up, picking his teeth. He seemed upset.

'Leave alone,' said Karim.

'Why cuz, don't tell me you're getting all fucking emotional on me, mate?'

'Na.'

'Then what cuz?'

'Karim never able to wipe ass properly.'

Buster laughed.

'Well fuck the yummy mummy, no shit. Don't tell me you wash it with Vodka?' I asked.

'How to know?'

'Just a wild shot in the fucking dark, mate. Now, go back to sleep. Pablo, this is your carnival, if you want to take a one-hour shit and wash you ass, then fucking go for it.'

'You are truly good spirit gringos. I love you all.'

'Ok fuck off then Brah.'

Now that we'd gotten rid of Pablo, we could all walk around the carnival and have some fun. I mean, why come to a carnival of fun if you can't have fun, ay? Anyway, that was my too fucking right philosophy, and if the powers that be didn't like it, I'd show em' my mean side, mate.

'And remember,' said Pablo with his head in the side window, 'if you don't want to work here, I'll call Tex, and he'll shove all of his 52 stars so far up your ass that you'll recite the national anthem in a D major fart fest. You got it gringos?'

'Eshay, what the fuck, brah? Me and Limmy ain't working. We're just here for crowd control brah.'

'Ok then, you two come with me.'

'No fuk wipe.'

'Yeah, ok, I can wipe my own ass, no problem gringo. Vince and Karim, you report to the Ferris wheel. Timmy will show you the ropes.'

We walked around the carnival looking for the Ferris

wheel. I left it to Karim to let me know where it was.

'Ya know cuz, big circle thing that goes around, almost a fucking hundred feet tall?'

'Yeah, there is. Timmy in the box.'

We waited outside for 5 minutes, peering in like perverts. He was doing paperwork of some kind, looking at this magazine, turning it upside down and sideways all the time. We couldn't see what it was, but it must have been really fucking interesting.

Just when we turned our backs, he jumped out of his little box and slid on the grass in front of us. It was either his shoes or he had plenty of fucking energy.

'Hey, bozos, losers, stale crinkle cut chips, what are your sorry asses doing in my neighborhood?' asked Timmy.

'Pablo's orders cuz, we're here to learn the ropes.'

Timmy asked if we were related. When I said no, he looked really disappointed.

'What do you mean ropes?' he asked. 'All grease-driven gears and sexy hydraulics here, my lavender friends. You wanna see?'

'Oh yes, fucking please cuz, it's what I live for.'

'Don't be a smart-ass, or I'll ship you back to Rock Central.'

Rock Central?? Fuck me, cuz, the guy knew where I came from. I reckon Veronica had him on the blower just before we came. Told him all about the Lebbo world and all its magnificence. I reckon he was the luckiest bastard in the carnival, mate, really fucking privileged to know about my missile-driven, insanely demented, siren-loving culture.

'Why Rock Central?' I asked. I wanted to know for sure.

'You got rocks in your pants. Down there.'

'Na mate, you got it all wrong cuz, I just got big balls ay. We stock more cum in Lebbo land than the Hamesh store wheat in winter. Plenty of fluid in these two beauties, my friend.'

I yanked my pants so he could see my oval style egg demons from hell.

'Wow, now that's a cream pie definition of talent, I must admit. What's your secret?' asked Timmy.

'Well, cuz, it's an ancient tradition, I'm not sure I can tell ya. The mighty Allah just may smack me over the head when I finally get to paradise.'

'Oh, come on, brunette baby, let me have it,' he said, clenching his fists.

'Well, we spend two weeks trying to find a tree amongst all the Rocky Mountains, then we whack our balls against it until they swell. We do this four times a day for a week cuz.'

'And then?'

'And then, my carnival friend, they become fluid spilling party balloons for the babes to enjoy.'

Karim just stood there looking stupid. He wasn't buying it, mate. He knew when I was spinning a yarn.

'Now that I've taught you a trade Muslim secret from the back end of the Quran, it's your time to teach us a skill. I want my Mum to be proud of me cuz.'

'Woo, you still live with your Mum?'

'I wish mate, I haven't seen her for fuck knows how long. I wanna make her proud, mate.'

Karim looked sad. I brought Timmy to one side.

'Aw shit, don't talk too much about Mums, mate.

Karim lost his in all the KGB paperwork.'

'You're the one who brought it up, you dumb shit, and you haven't shut up about anything and everything since we met, and that was only five minutes ago. Looks like I'd better teach you something.'

Timmy led us into the control box.

'Now,' he said with one hand on his hip, 'You pull the lever down to turn off the safety. When carriage number 12 gets to the top, you press the red button to stop so everyone gets a view, then green to go, get it?'

'Hmm…Red means to go, and green is no. The lever is good when up to down,' said Karim.

'Good! I'm off to the bog house to help out Pablo, he's getting old and needs a hand.'

I felt like a celebrity, all wired up and hammered to wreak fun on people. I had the red and green buttons at my fingertips and a hot rod lever to jerk at my command. I was glamming it all up cuz, like a Lebbo orgy with vodka cocktails out the back, ready to meet and greet everyone into my new love nest of fun.

'Aw yeah, little family, get in ay? It's good to see ya, Mum, cuz, and it's great you've still got a figure after all those kids. What's she like in bed Dad? Still popping like the first time, mate?'

I reckon they thought it was part of an act mate, like a dingo with baby clothes in its mouth running away from a campsite, so I kept the Wog shit going thick and fast.

'Ok, Karim, were you listening to Tommy about these controls?'

'He name Timmy.'

'Yeah, what the fuck ay. Were you listening or not?'

'Buttons to go, levers to blow, you know?'

'Right, I hear ya, so we press both buttons ten seconds apart?'

'Huh? Yeah ok. Pull lever down.'

In no time, those families were screaming with joy. The carriages were rocking like Elvis on uppers, and that stop-start motion was getting everyone pumping. I could see hands waving out the doors, babies shitting their pants, and grandma canes smashing at the back windows. The whole scene was like a drive-in theatre shag, fucking the night away in the back seat of a red Monaro drinking green ginger wine. All that was missing was George Thorogood on high, really fucking high.

'Hang on, stop,' said Karim.

'Why, we're on a roll cuz.'

'Timmy said number 12 on top, stop.'

'And then we walk?'

'I guess.'

I flicked the lever when carriage number 12 was high and dry at the top, then picked myself up and fucked off with Karim close behind me. There had to be something more entertaining than sprogging shit on decent, well-mannered families at high altitudes, like putting ping-pong balls in a clown's mouth, cuz. Yes, that was it, the most entertaining activity on the planet, the holy fucking grail of pleasure and entertainment, mate. Just the thought of picking up a well-manicured white ping pong ball and actually placing it in the mouth of a clown made me cum in my pants, and with my extra-sized Lebbo balls, I packed a load of cream larger than Grandpa Cadbury in his prime.

'I don't like clowns,' said Karim.

'Fuck mate, you made a full English sentence

without fucking it up, well done.'

'I said, I no to like clowns.'

'Well, that didn't last long, did it? Back to the usual KGB fuckup show? It's all good my skid-marked friend, I'm with ya. I'll even pass the ping pong balls from left to right and hold your hand like a grinning chimpanzee, and if the clown's start talking in English, I'll let ya know.'

We stood in front of those hungry clowns, looking left and right as they did. It was kinda hypnotic cuz, like they were looking for something that never fucking appeared. Or perhaps they were just fed up with their current occupation? Maybe I was reading too much into the situation.

As interesting as those lifeless clowns were, logging up points to win a furry critter made in a crowded Sri Lankan garage by abused children, our eyes were firmly set on the Ferris wheel. Some dipshit had left all the passengers stranded with a little kid in charge pressing buttons at will.

Not long after, Timmy passed by us smelling like a sheep station, sniffing at his hands like a tribal boy relying on paperbark to wipe the almighty brown from a peach-like surface. When he arrived at the Ferris Wheel, the ride-goers kicked the shit outa him on the grass. We thought about coming over to help, but those clowns had us captivated mate, really fucking enthused to the max, cuz. It was like the strongest glue thought up in all of mankind's bonding experiments.

Impressing Mum on the north shore was looking better by the minute, mate. I'd gained a qualification in Ferris wheel controls and mastered the excitement of clowns forever turning their heads with no outcome in mind.

'Oy! Gringos, get over here. Over here Gringos!' said a familiar voice at the merry-go-round.

We walked slowly towards the bloke, weary of his shit-clad hands that we could see from the clown station. We felt sorry for the bloke cuz, but hey, who wants to hang around someone who smells like shit cuz? It's just not practical. He extended his hand as soon as we arrived.

'Hey Pablo shit cuz, I mean, cool dude, howdy mate,' I said with my hands in the air.

Karim pretended to pick at his pimples with both hands.

'I hear you fucked up everything you touched today,

Gringos? Timmy is in hospital after sixteen people kicked the shit out of him on the lawn. You know anything about that?'

'Ah, define know, cuz?'

Karim's face started to bleed.

'Well, it's not exactly our fault cuz. We just wanted to impress our Mums, ya know? Don't you have a Mum mate, all the way back home where all the poor people live, or does your family have an opioid plantation?'

'Hey Gringo, don't push the white powder industry, eh? The packages that drop from the sky put most teenagers through college in this country. Who could afford caviar without us, eh? Anyway, that doesn't change the fact that you two are a pair of natural-born fuckups. Hey, what's Karim doing in that stall window?'

I looked over at one of the tents and saw Karim fighting with the owner.

We rushed over to see what all the fuss was about, cuz.

'She, Nikita, how much sells?' asked Karim.

'Excuse me, sir, we do not sell dress mannequins at

any price. Can you please let go?'

'Karim, Russian pal! What the fuck is going on, cuz?'

'She is Nikita, my lost love. Must have her.'

He'd mistaken his old girlfriend for a dress mannequin with a fur coat and ug boots. He must have been drunk, mate.

'Hey, dickhead, it's a doll mate, a fucking plastic toy to display clothes. Don't ya get it?'

'Hey, it's ok,' said Pablo, slapping me on the back, 'Maybe he likes that kind of thing, ya know? Some people like the doll with rubber tits. After all, it doesn't talk back, eh Gringo?' he said, laughing.

'It's not funny, Pablo, and I'm not lugging this fucking thing around Sydney! It's embarrassing, mate!'

'So true Gringo.'

Karim began to cry as the shop lady dragged Nikita out the back. It was obvious that Karim needed help with the lady talk, and I was obviously the one to teach him. A well-oiled dialogue expert from the land of rocky roads and AK-47 rifles.

Chapter Four

We met Tex and Veronica in the car park, and I could tell they'd heard the news by the look on their faces. I knocked on the back window a few times, but they ignored me. I wasn't sure if they could see me through the illegal tinting, so I head-butted the roof a few times. I reckon I had it over Tex by that stage, but maybe I was just getting cocky.

'Get off the car, you Ohio River half-cast maggot!' screamed Tex from inside the car.

He had all the lines, mate. Sometimes, I thought of him as the main character of a book or something. Fucking real-life superhero, cuz!

Suddenly, the back window came down an inch, and Veronica handed me a note. She'd been crying, and I thought it might have had something to do with me.

As I held it up, a wind blew across me, and the paper went sailing, so I banged on the window again.

'Jesus, sorry Veronica, that note looked really fucking important ay, nice handwriting and even smelt of perfume, mate. You're a real fucking class act, cuz.'

'Get the fuck in here, Wog boy, you too, Russian!'

We drove ten metres due north, where Limmy was waiting in a parked car.

'Right, go with Limmy on a bubble bath deal to glory. I can't trust your pair of fuckups to get anything done properly by yourselves. If you're lucky, you might learn a thing or two about business deals and the way the USA runs the world. Limmy can explain the details. Now the get the fuck out?' screamed Tex.

Veronica didn't say a thing, but that was ok, as her boring white girl chitchat dulled my senses no end, cuz. I liked her body though.

'Limmy there,' said Karim.

'Yeah, I fucking know, mate. I saw the car when we arrived. It's only 10 metres away.'

'Jim fuk lover!' he screamed from the driver's side window.

We both jumped in the back to distance ourselves from the usual red duck banter, but there was no escaping it all mate. His interior was decorated with Chinese tattoos, tigers, and dragons - some crouching, others hidden. He had three meat cleavers hanging from his revision mirror, and the door handles were crab claws hardened with resin, so every time I went to open the door, I cut my hand. Really fucking well thought ay mate.

'So Limmy, ya Peking style take away container, where the fuck are we going?'

'Lentil can bugger in store of dark minds. Money rum boy!'

'Well, I don't have any more questions. How about you, Karim?'

'He shit me.'

'Fucking oath cuz.'

We drove for two minutes and stopped in front of a large factory.

'Sim card, bang boy, go inside.'

When we got to the front door, we saw a giant tin of beetroot on the ground that had fallen off its perch above the entrance. We sidestepped, not really knowing what to make of it. It was better not to say anything.

'Chum fucker clever!'

Limmy began to hack into the can, which was made of cardboard with a politician's face on the front. We wondered if he knew the guy.

'Open the door and ask for help Karim. This ramen style halfwit is out of control cuz.'

From the look on the receptionist's face, I thought we'd fucked it all up from the word go. She was standing tall, watching Limmy hack into the giant can of beets with a meat clever outside. She asked us if we knew the guy, and we replied 'no fucking way' at the same time.

'Lock the door, will ya love. That's a good boy,' she said.

Jesus, mate, she talked like a granny. A nice blonde with tits like Sammy Fox.

We explained that Tex had sent us for work experience, winking all the while so she'd get it.

'Excuse me, dear, are you winking at me?'

'Yeah, bubble bath deal for Tex,' whispered Karim.

'I see. Give me one moment, please.'

She disappeared for five minutes and came back with a smile on her face.

'I'm sorry, dear, but we are not purchasing any new

sanitary products this year. We have plenty of soap and lavender left over but thank you.'

'No, you dumb old scag, we're here on Tex's orders, ya know, bubble bath shit, right, darl, ya know?'

The old duck looked horrified cuz, like I'd just grabbed a feather duster and swept the cobwebs from between her legs.

'I'm calling security!'

'Yeah, I'll give ya security, babe. Can I have your number?'

Just then, a six-foot Māori lad burst through the door.

'Hey, cuz, you need to move on, ay?'

'Excuse me, are you trying to talk like me, cuz?' I asked.

'Na way cuz boy, this is how we talk in New Zealand ay, swear to god cuz.'

Karim looked at us and did a double-take.

'You're stealing my show, ya fat fuck. It's me and you, to the death!' I said.

'Yeah, cuzzina, you and who's a plantation of kiwi fruit, cuz?'

'Don't fuck with me haka lover. I'm a badass boy in Lebanon with a big reputation. Look at the size of my balls!'

I gave myself a forward pants yank and showed him my goods. Those swollen camel toes did the trick.

'There ya go, island lad, c'mon make a move. Jesus, you're fatter than fuck!' I said, moving around like a boxer.

'Now hang on, let's settle this without pain, cuz.'

'Say that word one more time, and I'll order Limmy inside.'

By this time, the secretary was hiding under the desk.

'Anyway, what business do you have in a beetroot factory?' he asked with a croaky voice.

'Ay, beets, not lentils?' asked Karim.

'Lentil heaven is next door, ya dumb fuck!' said the Māori boy.

'Aw yeah, that's why Limmy is hacking into the can outside. Shit, sorry, cuz and cuzzina, we'll just head next door then, shall we?'

'Fuck up, man,' said Karim.

By the time we got outside, Limmy had hacked the beet can into a thousand pieces.

'Jesus, cuz, you knew this was the wrong place. Why didn't you tell us, mate?'

'New clever, test swishy fuck. Limited English.'

So, we walked next door and did the same thing we did at the beet company, minus the Limmy act of cold-blooded dissection. This time, there actually was an old bag at reception that talked and walked like an old bag, so it made me feel better.

'Ah yeah, old bag, any chance you've heard of Tex at all? I checked the sign at the door, and it said Lentil Heaven, and Limmy isn't pissed to be here.'

'Excuse me? You may address me as Agatha!'

'Ay yeah, Aggy, whatever, just say Tex's boys are here to the big boss.'

'I used to be head Nun at my old convent, you know. I despise young tyrants like you with bad attitudes and filthy mouths.'

'What about balls like these ay grandma?'

I did the whole front pants strauss again and put my big boys right in front of her. She went pale, ay mate, real fucking pale.

She pulled out a big stick and came at me with it, mate, swinging left and right like an expert swordsman. Even Limmy was scared.

'Hay man, what's all the commotion man, like, there's a great disturbance in the universe or something,' said a voice from a nearby office.

'I'm sorry, Mr. Velkman. I'm just dealing with something,' said the old duck.

'Hey mate, you know Tex cuz?' I screamed.

A long-haired lay about peered through an open door, his left eye going one way, the other looking straight ahead.

'Say again, man?'

'Tex, you heard of him, mate?'

'Yeah.'

'So let us in cuz. We're the men of the moment, the angels a few, mate.'

'Tex said a stupid Lebbo idiot, a lonely Russian, and a clever wielding manic was going to help me out today.'

'That's us, cuz, you got it, mate. Can we come in?'

'No!' said the old duck.

'It's ok, Agg., my neglected love child. We can work it out. Send them through to my garden of wisdom.'

Fuck, this guy had me in a trance. I was hoping to score some dope before the day was finished. But I just wanted to make a little progress, cuz. I mean, fuck me, I could still see Timmy across the road from the front door, all bandaged up, manning the Ferris wheel, mate.

I almost choked when we arrived at his office, mate. The smell of lemon grass mixed with cannabis, hippy deodorant, and a pot of lentil soup on the stove made me dry reach. Limmy walked over to the soup and stirred it with his meat clever, and Karim sat on the floor playing with his pubic hair again. It was hard for anyone to take us seriously, I reckon, with me being the exception, all prim and well-mannered like ay?

'So, are you the head dick man?' he asked.

'Yeah, I got a dick and big pair of balls to go with it,

mate.'

'Na man, the boss?'

'Almost. I just need to get rid of that American pecan pie that keeps yelling at me, then score his bird so I can get some well-earned trim. Then, yeah, I'll be the boss.'

'My birth name is Rumpole. I honour all gods but the one you do. Is that a problem?'

'The one I do? What, you got ESP powers, mate? What the fuck are ya talking about?'

'It's just a way to start a convo, man, like sharing a new brand of tea, ya know?'

'Um, yeah.'

'Tex, tell ya why you're here?'

'To learn, mate, to upskill in this modern world of bullshit, to get ahead, conquer and divide. All that shit, yeah?'

'You need some bad green leaf, man. Here, grab an end and copy me.'

He grabbed a short hose connected to a vase that was burning the good stuff. It had eight hoses going off in different directions, cuz.

In and out, we breathed until Karim grabbed it off me and went for it himself. Limmy was mixing bubble bath into the lentil soup, so we didn't bother him. By no time, the whole office was chock full of smoke.

'Put the air-con on man. Just to the right.'

Karim stumbled around, knocking all the pot plants over.

'Easy, man, Dad will be here soon. We need to have a meeting about our mission.'

Karim suddenly got the air-con to work, and it sucked all the smoke out.

'Mission?' I asked with bloodshot eyes.

'We've got work to do, my natural pest-free pedigree chums. It's all part of what Budda has in store for us.'

'You work, Dad?' asked Karim.

'I work what?' he replied.

'Work Dad?

'Do I work him man?'

'No work fuck chuck?' replied Limmy.

'No, he works for his father, fuck me, am I the only

person in this room who speaks English?' I said.

'Don't swear man. Mother nature hates it.'

Couldn't argue with that.

'Mr. Rumpole, your father is here,' blared the old duck on the intercom.

'Ah man, it's the old man, man. It's Dad, man.'

'Aw, what a fucking surprise, cuz. Your Dad is a man. Really fucking insightful, mate.'

Rumpole began to clean up, throwing things around the room as if they would magically go back to where they belonged. He pressed on the intercom a few times.

'Aggy, Aggy man, the old man is coming, help Aggy babe.'

'Coming Mr. Velkman!'

When Agatha got inside, she knew just what to do, like it was second nature to the old duck. She really knew her stuff. It was like watching Mum vacuum under my feet in complete fucking awe, mate. What a worker, what a champ.

'Will there be anything else, Mr. Velkman?'

'You're not gonna stay, Aggy?' asked Rumpole.

'Now you know your father doesn't like me in the meetings, Rumpole. Just smile and speak your mind.'

'Cheer up, cuz, at least you know it's about Lentils, mate. No big surprises, ay cuz?'

Two minutes later, the fattest fuck you've ever seen squished through the door. I watched him wriggle like an elephant seal hooked on chocolate ice cream, and when his ass hit the sofa, a puff a dust rose to the ceiling.

'You, son, speak to me dearest,' he said.

'Um, yes, Dad.'

He sat there waving his finger in the air, catching his breath like a geriatric with asthma.

'No, no, young man. About the shipment. How are the boys here going?'

'Haven't told em, Dad. They just got here.'

'Ah, yes, well, my global friends. A sample from everywhere I see. That's nice, I like that. Diversity in all its grandeur.'

'Shit cuz, you speak nice ay.'

'Educated, born and bred in the bosom of England,

my chum. Outsmarted the cleverest of them I have, agree, son?'

'Yeah man.'

'Ah yes, man this, man that. How he got this way, I'll never know. God knows his mother was a scholar and read a thousand books a year.'

'Shut up, Dad, you're making me look bad in front of the fellas.'

'Kim fuk Sally.'

'Um, he agrees,' I said quickly.

'It seems the Chinese boy has talent. What's with the meat clever?'

'Stir fuk nice. Blubber lok chum choy?' said Limmy, looking Rumpole's dad up and down.

'Excuse me?' he asked.

'Um, I think he wants you to try some lentil soup?' I answered.

Limmy stood there twirling his meat clever ay, looking at those tender, blubberish tuck shop arms, swaying with every syllable he uttered mate.

'Right now, Tex has asked me to take you lot on. I'm a little hesitant, but I need your expertise. We ship cans of lentils to every corner of the globe, but recently, business has been a little slow, my boys.'

'Great cuz, so you've got time to relax and get more out of life, mate?'

'Um, no, I didn't mean that. It's about money, my friend, and that's the bottom line.'

'Yeah, the line, man, you see what it comes to? All this universal bullshit that comes together, like a billion shards of light exploding then reassembling again. It all comes back to us, man, you see?' said Rumpole.

'Yes, so, hearing that codswallop, can you see why you three will come in handy? I believe your expertise will be invaluable to this company.'

Geeze, mate, I dunno what Tex told this guy, but I reckon he was jumping to conclusions, mate. I mean, I'm a pretty cluey fella, but Karim and Limmy need help, mate, really fucking serious intervention, cuz. He'll find out.

After a feed of lentils laced with bubble bath and stainless-steel meat clever filings, we walked across to an old storage shed with broken windows. There were boxes piled upon boxes like a forklift driver had nothing else to do but fuck with the hydraulics sniffing white powder.

'Now, before you, good sirs, are three hundred boxes of quality lentils from the bosom of the NSW countryside. They are shipped to the Middle East, where they eat them like peanuts.'

'You mean Lebanon cuz?'

'Yes, right you are my young employee. And they are going directly at the seaport in Beirut. Your job is to … well, my son will go into the details, but they need repacking as such.'

'Hey man? I don't remember that part, Dad.'

'Oh, for god's sake, son, when will you take your sight off the almighty universe and focus on something practical?'

'You mean like lentils?'

The old man was beginning to sweat.

'Yes, like fucking lentils cuz, a speck in the universe that you can actually do something with besides stare at?' I said.

'Shut up man! In a roundabout, holistic way, I'm technically your boss, so peep down.'

The old fella went into an office and brought out a square package and a small wooden box.

'Oh yeah, man, that's right, the white lady, yes, I remember, man.'

'That's good, son, and what do we do with the white lady?'

'Stick it in, man, right in tight at the bottom.'

'Yes, very good, you put the package underneath the lentils in one of these small wooden boxes. Understand everyone?'

'So, we're shipping bubble bath in boxes with lentils cuz?'

'Oh yes, how strikingly humorous, bubble bath, my gosh, how delightful!'

He and Karim began to laugh, a mixture of one of those sneaky fucking Russian laughs, and an old fat fuck who talked to Mary Poppins in his sleep.

'Ok, so it's bubble bath as usual with a lentil twist?

We can do that cuz.'

'Splendid, absolutely splendid, my boys. You have five hours to box everything up, then drive the shipment to Darling Point Wharf. No stuffing this up, Rumpole, you hear? I'm leaving you in charge.'

The big fella left in a blaze of glory, sliding like a well-fed snail out the door at a hundred miles an hour. Five minutes later, we got to work.

'Dam lentil boy dim sim shit.'

'I agree, Limmy, ay? Let me do the organising, ay cuz?'

'Na man, Dad said I'm in charge man, don't fuck with the boss karma situation fellas.'

'Whatta you think, Karim?' I asked, looking around the shed.

'Office dog shit mut,' pointed Limmy.

Karim was dragging out boxes of bubble baths from the office. He'd decided that small talk wasn't going to help, even though he was the master of two-word sentences that dribbled out the corner of his mouth like early morning geriatric custard.

'Na man, not on the bottom, man. It'll crush the love powder, man.'

And the lentil lady was right, cuz. We had to think of something really fucking clever, or the bubble would turn to rubble.

'Just put it on top man! With some packing bubble.'

'That's fucking good, cuz! Bubble on bubble! You must have a goddamn IQ of 360?'

'Thanks man! Tell Dad that. He thinks I'm a small-town pervert who peers into kiddies windows at midnight, man.'

'Did he say?' asked Karim.

'Na, but I can read minds, man, ya know, like extra telepathy stuff, looking into the blackness of wherever and getting good information, ya know, man?'

We ignored him and set up a factory lineup system. Limmy opened the boxes with his meat clever, Rumpole wrapped the bubble bath, Karim placed it on top of the lentils, and I taped-up the box. In a few hours, we were packed and ready to load.

'Get the truck, man, can ya?'

'You talking to me cuz?

'Yeah, man, Dad said you had a license.'

'Me drive,' said Karim.

Before we all knew it, Karim was in the driver's seat, ready to roll, cuz. He had the gears and clutch all sorted. I was really fucking impressed.

'There are times when you don't make me sick, ay cuz. You're a fucking sickle-assed legend today, my man.'

Things were tight with all four of us jammed in the front seat. The wharf was only one hour away, but it took us two, as we had to stop for petrol. Karim demanded that we pay for the petrol in four equal shares, with three IOUs submitted immediately. That meant Rumpole had to pay by default. Who said the sneaky fucking Russian was all stale Vodka and no brain cells? He was impressing me more by the minute, but I knew that would change when a full English sentence was required. Not knocking the bloke or anything, it's just plain fucking reality.

'Left deep fry but,' said Limmy, pointing with his meat cleaver.

'You mean right cuz? I can see water that way?'

'Ya black duck,' he replied with a nod.

'Ok then, right, no left, hang on, we're here, mate. Turn off the engine.'

I was right into the orders cuz, like I was the head dick of ball central, giving all the directions for the love juice to follow. I was giving myself gold stars, real fucking bright ones, mate.

'Get out, man, and wait on the seat over there. I know the captain, and he knows me.'

'That helps cuz, or is it the other way around?'

'Wait at the seat, man, and I'll talk to the captain.'

We waited there like three ducks in a snake pit, all fidgety cuz, like there was something going on behind the scenes.

'Yeah, man, I understand, but do your recycling first, man, ya know, like a good citizen and all that jizz.'

'I am to report to my Captain in the Philippines, not you!' cried the boat captain.

He'd come all the way from the Philippines to do this special bubble bath run, cuz. I could read the guy's lips from my seat. He was talking about living it up in Manilla, having sixteen wives, and shagging them all at the same time. I was pretty fucking good at the old lip-reading mate, two hundred percent accuracy on a rainy day with skid-marked jocks on. I was about to find out, as the lentil boy was on his way over.

'Captain Ladyboy wants to do his recycling before we load up. That set us back an hour, man.'

'Kim wait fuk dog!'

Limmy was right. The longer we hung around, the greater chance the cops would notice our suspicious activity cuz, even more so than us dickheads sitting on a bench trying to be casual. We were all so fucking different.

'Hey, budda, you got smoke?' said a stinky fella from behind me.

He was an African guy with yellow teeth, or perhaps a native from an island. Definitely not Hungarian or Egyptian.

'So, you're English then, cuz?' I asked.

'Yeah, bud, real English, ay budda. You fucking blind?'

'Aw yeah, native Aussie, you guys are untouchable mate, right away from the tear me down shit ay cuz? You're the first one I've met ay. None of you on the north shore, cuz.'

'Me Jimmy from Redfern. You got a university degree?'

'Of course, can't you tell by the way I talk, mate?'

'Piss off, Budda, you immigrant like them. Me got badge, see.'

And it wasn't a boy scout badge with Humphry Bear stuck in the middle. The bloke was a cop mate, a full true blue black one.'

'Hey, sorry, Mr. Luther King! Pardon me manners, cuzzina. These are my mates, Limmy, Rumpole, and Karim. Have you seen us before? We're famous.'

'Famous in own mind Buddah?' asked Jimmy.

'Aw, King, cuz mate, can I call you that, Mr. King?'

'So, all black fellas talk in a park to 250,000 people in the middle of summer about stupid dream?'

He was stoned on Kava, mate, I was sure of it.

'Anyway Buddahs, you see the Philippine captain over there, the one diving into the sea to get away?'

'Sure, man, he said he was doing his recycling, man.'

'Na budda, he's hiding his woomera between his legs and tuck tailing round the Roo course. He knows who I am, do you?'

'Cop slag?'

'Close, I work for the DDA.'

'Of course, man, hold the lentils in boxes, mate, oops, I mean, the phone, man.'

'Hah, so that's how you do the dirt track marathon with bare feet, Budda? I'll take a look inside with my artificial spear if you don't mind?'

'Go man, don't care, man. Dad's coming anyway, oops!'

The dirt track copper looked in the back of our truck and found the boxes.

'Wood thing, like the tree, like a spear, like a woomera, like…' said Jimmy.

'Give it a fucking rest cuz. Just open the boxes.'

'Huh?' said Rumpole.

'Aw, I mean no, I mean don't open the fucking things cuz, aw sorry man, I meant the opposite,' I yelled, jumping up and down on the park bench.

'You lot look sus ay, like a camera with lens cap on,' said Jimmy.

He opened the first box and found the bubble bath.

'Ok lentil schemers, you and all your cooktop chefs are coming out bush with me,' said Jimmy.

'Where man?'

'To the lock-up!'

We all piled into the copper's car and drove downtown. He called through to his boss and asked for a spare swinging dick to come out and confiscate the truck. I felt like taking a shit.

'Fuck me, anyone feel like taking a shit cuz?'

Everyone held up their hand, including the copper.

'Thanks for the tip. I've been wanting a shit for two weeks. Usually, I rub up and down on a bark tree and force it out, but everything is concrete here,' said Jimmy.

'So, you only shit in the woods, man?' asked Rumpole.

'Just like a bear, Budda, but I do like David Jones, always shit there. Something about the atmosphere, Budda, like as soon as I get on the escalator, the shit drops straight from me ass. I have to hold it in with one finger, so I don't *rip it* right there on the conveyor steps.'

None of us had anything to say to that cuz. Totally un-fucking commentable.

'So, anyone else for a shit?' asked the copper in front of David Jones.

'Na, only one person at a time can bog on a shit hole, man, don't you know that?' said Rumpole.

Jimmy shook his head and ducked into David Jones for a ripper session. He left the engine running with the door open, and we all just stared at each other. By the time he returned half an hour later, we'd only just started planning our getaway.

'Feel better, man?' asked Rumpole.

'Na budda, lots of farting and false hope. Even got my finger in there for a swish, but still no tribal movement.

Now, let's get you crew to the lock-up.'

The fingerprinting at the lock up went well, like art classes when I was a young Lebbo preschooler on the North Shore, cuz. The lady copper babe was cute ay, especially in that tight uniform with her hair up, all for me, of course, and my fucking irresistible manner-like charm. I thought I was in for a minute, right up until she bent my arm behind my back and threw me in the cell with the rest of the crew. Limmy was allowed to keep his meat clever after he somehow got hold of some peanut butter and jammed it up his arse, then licked his fingers clean in front of the officers. No one would go near him, cuz.

'Jesus, officer babe. He's got a meat-clever baby. You're a sworn officer, baby, cuz. Do Something,' I asked the lock-up chick.

She stood there, watching Limmy lick his fingers clean, then take another grab from his yellow tainted ass and feast some more. We all fucking dry-reached, mate. Fucking disgusting behavior, even for us bubble bath crew.

'You really know how to work a system, Limmy, fucking hats off to your prawn chips.'

'Butter crack, hit the sack.'

And he was right. Everyone in the cell was fucked, so Rumpole and Karim curled up next to me, and Limmy slept as far away as possible cuz.

'Wake up, you're the voice Buddha, try and understand it!' yelled a familiar voice.

Only he knew what that meant.

'Come out, Buddas. You're free to go.'

'It's 3 a.m., man. Turm of the fucking lentil lights love child.'

'Your tests are negative. Fucking rubber duck tea time in the lab ay? You pear-shaped gorillas make fun of us coppers?'

'Ay Cuz?'

'The whole forensic lab is full of bubbles. Are you corroboree dropouts messing with us? The whole fucking truck was full of boxes with true blue bubble bath cases in them, Budda. You wasted our time.'

Jimmy walked off before we could think of anything to say.

'Lucky, ay man? Real bubble bath. My dad must have known, man. He'll have an explanation.'

We stood out in the street at 4:30am and sang Christmas carols with our hands outstretched. When some crazy cuz gave Rumpole a dollar, he used it to call his dad to find out what the fuck happened.

'Huh, what Dad? Whatta ya mean you don't trust me?'

Rumpole kept saying the same thing over and over until the money ran out.

'Prick doesn't trust me, man. Used us as a decoy man.'

'Smart cock,' said Limmy, still licking the chunky spread from his fingers.

'Let's get some early breakfast, guys, my shout,' said Rumpole.

'No money cock sack,' replied Limmy.

Rumpole pulled out a neatly folded fifty-dollar bill from his sock.

'Be prepared, man, that's what the scouts say.'

'You went to fucking scouts cuz? Did you get strung up on the flagpole?'

'You want some lentil soup, man? I'm the only one

with love cash, honey.'

'So why didn't you tell us that before we sung Christmas carols for an hour in the middle of July dickhead?' I asked.

Karim laughed.

We all sat at the Piss-Pot café at different tables. Limmy still had love fudge on his fingers, Karim was crying about his Mum, and Rumpole was washing his hair with water from the flower vase. I was the only sane one in the group cuz, sitting nicely with a porn mag I'd found on the ground. It had most of the pages stuck together and a funny smell to it, but I battled on and tried to salvage what I could. When the baked beans and coffee came, I hoed in before I had a chance to wash my hands. Always too many things to remember, cuz!

'Nikita, I miss you, Nikki, mama lady,' cried Karim from the far table.

'I thought she was your lost love, cuz? Are you pissed or something?'

'Same name as mother,' he cried.

It was then that I noticed a dozen shots of Vodka on his table. He hadn't ordered a bite to eat, and with all that booze on an empty stomach, he was going downhill fast, cuz. It was lucky the waitress was a soft lass cuz, or she'd have made a complaint. Instead, she let Karim call her Nikita and go through her handbag looking for miniature missiles.

'Hey, little Russian. There are no missiles in my handbag, dear. My name is Slovak, if you must know,' said the waitress.

'Slovak? that my sister's name. Are you her?'

'Ah, no, and don't pull on my leg. Can I get some help here, please?'

'Ah, he's just playing around, Slovak, cuz. You remind him of his sister. Just humour him a little, can't you, babe, cuz?'

'Well, he's already got his hand on my ass and his tongue in my belly button. Do all Russians do this to their sister?'

'What last name, baby, tell me, and I'll let go, promise,' said Karim.

'No, you can let me go now, please.'

He put his tongue back into her navel.

'Ok it's Putin. Are you happy? I married a Russian!'

'So, it's ok then? Russian can protect lonely woman with hammer and sickle.'

'No, he's an alcoholic and a womaniser.'

Karim let her go and set his sights on the bartender, who happened to be a shemale, but hey, cuz, who can tell from that distance?

'Well, if it isn't my old preacher porn loving fun, grand maneuver crew of disastrous proportions,' said Tex from the café doorway. Veronica was standing next to him.

Everyone froze, like standing to attention but sitting down.

'You, hippy-loving dog shit, go home to your fat fuck daddy and tell him to call me, ya hear?'

'Ok Tex man, see ya fellas. I love you.'

Karim looked sad.

'Limmy, catch a cab and meet Buster at my house. There's a deal happening at midday. Take care of it for me, will ya?'

'Deal done duck.'

We all converged at one table.

'Well, it looks like congratulations are in order. You rancid tailbone shit lickers sure made me proud. The fat fuck told me you moved the whole shipment without a single cop coming at ya. Is that right? Now don't lie to me, ya hear?'

Karim nodded.

'Well, if that don't take the ice-cream from an orphan child. Fucking impressive, my wholehearted reject friends. I'm so fucking impressed, I'm gonna send you to the gym to get some real-life career experience.'

'Gym cuz?'

'You're gonna learn to be boxers, and all that goes with the profession. There's plenty to learn there, from fight fixing to reading the odds. You heard of Shorty's Gym?'

'Na,' replied Karim.

'Well, your gonna you self-indulgent belly button licker! Now, flag down Limmy and get him to drop you off. Here's fifty dollars each for your bubble bath victory. Now go on git, ya hear!'

Veronica started to play with Tex's belt again. She

had those hungry eyes, so we got up and split.

Chapter Five

The taxi ride into the city was a fucking nightmare. The window tint was pitch black, and the driver had satanic Perspex behind him. I thought I heard ghost noises at one stage, cuz. Limmy sat in the front seat with the driver and kept resetting his metre, so by the time we got there, he argued that the taxi hadn't moved. The driver was a fellow Lebbo, so he let us off after I promised I'd give him a piece of my grandma's insurance deal, which was now legendary in Lebanon. If I ever went back there, mate, I'd be mobbed in the streets cuz, like a fucking seriously famous golfer or a master chef that kept yelling at everyone because his parents got divorced and his Scottish father abused him or something.

'Kim, fuk ladies, get out!' cried Limmy as we arrived at Shorty's gym.

The place looked more like a paper stand than a gym, with old newspapers floating down the street and concert advertising splattered on the walls.

'Door fucked,' said Karim.

'Just wiggle it, mate. You gotta be tough at these joints, ay. These places are overrun by meat-headed, steroid-fed zombies cuz. There's probably some meat lover's pizza holding the door from the other side.'

And I was right.

'Hey, ya, what's with the lip, little fella? I'm trying to get out and buy a newspaper,' said a thick-set bloke on the other side of the door.

Karim let go of the handle, and the door flung open.

'Hey yo, it's you two. About time ya know, Shorty's been expecting you.'

'Shit we're famous cuz! Dig on this guy, Karim. We didn't even have to open the door, and he knew who we were, mate. It's like me in Lebanon all over again, burning prayer mats in the street and setting houses alight. It's too much, cuz?' I said, with my hands on me head.

'Will you shut the fuck up yo, and empty the sweat buckets. We've got boxers in here that need fresh water for sparring, ya know? The last ones got a little beaten up, so the agency said they'd send two more this morning. That's you two, right?'

'Sweat buckets? How does a boxer sweat that much?'

'It's a figure of speech, yo! The water and sweat are mixed to form a salty fluid. Now, are you guys coming in or what?'

'Sorry, to do what?'

He grabbed us by the collar and dragged us inside. Lucky Limmy wasn't there, or he'd be Italian spaghetti.

'Are you Italian?' I asked.

'Huh?'

'Well, you've got the whole rock the jive Italian Stallion thing going, ya know, Rocky Balboa mean street illiterate bonehead rapist kind of deal?'

He stood back like he was offended or something.

'Ah, yo, right. Did Shorty set this up? Ah, jee, that little fella. He's too much. Hey Shorty, you got a minute, yo?'

We looked over to where two boxers were sparring, and a short guy with grey hair popped his head out of nowhere.

'Yer wanna me Rock?'

'Yeah, yo Shorty, these two are the bucket boys. A couple of jokers, yo!'

It looked like he nodded his head, but he was so fucking short it was hard to tell.

'Bring em over ere, Rock!'

We walked over with the Italian fella nudging us from behind.

'Well, if it ain't the fellas I've been waiting for fur. Rock, meet, sorry, whatcha names?'

'Karim and Vince?'

'Ay yer, Tex's boys.'

'So, yo, these ain't the water boys?'

'Not yet, Rock. I'm taking them on as a special favour. Gonna teach em the ropes till they got speed!'

'You mean the whole chasing chickens on the road, yo? Where you totally humiliated me in front of a group of children and grandparents?'

'What the fuck yer talking about. You wanted speed,

didn't ya?'

'Ah yeah, yo, I guess, Shorty, but ya know, in front of the crowd like yo, I was a little embarrassed, you gotta understand, Shorty.'

'Understand this ya bolognaise bullshit hoarder, I'm yer trainer, got it? If you don't like it, you can go back to being a water boy.'

'Ay yeah cuz, he can do it, ay?'

'Shut yer mouth, or I'll send ya back to Tex with a note pinned to ya chest.'

I didn't ask for clarification.

'Rock, show 'em to their accommodation.'

'Yo right.'

Rock led us up two flights of stairs to an old room with cracked windows, insects on the ceiling and holes in the floorboards. Why did everything have to be so old in these places, cuz?

'This heaven compared to Russia.'

'Yeah, cuz?'

'When at home, I make cockroach bed on pillow next

to me. Call him name like a pet. It comes to me at night and strokes my cheek like this.'

He put his finger on my cheek and tickled me.

'You feel love, ok? It's nice to love,' said Karim.

'And that's why you dogs drink Vodka all day, hey? To take the pain away? Like your Mum used to?'

I knew I'd said the wrong thing, so I offered him the bed on the left, the one with no bedsheet and a torn blanket.

One hour later, I was in the ring with boxing gloves on while Karim held a bucket in the corner.

'Now, ya know why yer here?' asked Shorty.

'Not a fucking clue cuz!'

'Mind ya manners ya scurvy dog! You see all this around ya? Well?'

'Yeah, so?'

'This is tradition, son.'

'Yeah, I get it. Things that weren't here when the dinosaurs shat in the woods. Or was that a bear? Or does a bear shit in the woods? Karim, help me out here, mate?'

'Whose bear and where are the woods?'

'No, I mean the boxing stuff, ye dick brain! The gloves, the ring, the marks on the floor. The intermittent smells wafting from the men's changeroom.'

'It's a boxing gym, mate.'

Shorty lowered his head.

'Yo, Shorty, let me try. I can teach him some respect,' said Rock.

'You wanna piece of his ass, young fella?' asked Shorty.

'Yeah, cuz I reckon. I'm pretty fit, mate. When I was young, I used to climb down 250-foot wells just to get a cup of water. I've thrown rocks at refugees for target practice, then sat with peasants on a boat for 12 weeks. I can handle him cuz, you bet.'

I stood there flat-footed in front of Rock, looking him in the eye. It then occurred to me that I should be dodging and weaving, mate, so I turned on the charm.

'C'mon, rock the sock with an extra-large limp cock,' I said, dancing around the ring.

Karim dropped his bucket full of water.

'Russian dog, clean it up, yo?' said Rock.

Karim sat down with his legs crossed.

'So, it's you and me, mate. Just this pedigree stonemason and an outdated Ferrari, ay? You're going down, cuz, real fast and with lots of painkillers at the ready when you wake up. I swear to God cuz, you are the fucking ass end of a chicken ready to be thrown in the bin, the shit end of the stick that no one wants, and the wet dog that accidentally got let into the house, your…'

Everything suddenly went dark. I thought I was back in the cab again with Karim and Limmy, sniffing at the door handles to get a faint sense of trim. I was swimming in dark water, just myself in a sea of nothing, cuz, and then I woke up with Shorty's face in mine.

'Yer a knockout kid, that's fer sure.'

Karim was still sitting in the corner with his legs crossed.

'Yo, little fella, I'm sorry ya know, ya just kept talking shit.'

'Don't apologize, Rock. It was a learning experience fer him. He'll get more of that before he's through here, I can tell ya.'

'So, did I slip, mate? Must have hit my head, ay cuz.

Fucking sore.'

'Karim, bring over the bucket, will yer.'

Empty.

'Aw shit, what are yer good fer? Rock, go and get a glass of water.'

'Well, ya know, Shorty, I kinda got my gloves on, you know.'

'Then you look to the gods for answers, Rock, ask the hard questions yer never ask anyone, and if they don't tell ya the truth, come back, and I'll tell ya to take ya fucking gloves off before you pour the water!'

'Hey Shorty, that's brilliant yo, you're a god damn genius.'

I felt better after a few cups of water, so we all went for a run and left Shorty in the gym. Damn little runt pissed me off no end, like a midget wanker who couldn't make up his mind what he wanted out of life, so he chose to annoy others, hoping they would hand out the answers. These people really shave my scrotum, cuz. I'd get him later.

'Karim, why are you wearing leg warmers?' I asked.

'Keep legs warm.'

A few kilometres into the run, some kids started to run alongside us. It seemed like they knew Rock personally, chanting his name like a god, cuz. At first, I thought they were giving out girly likes to Karim and his bright white leg warmers.

Rock quickened the pace and left us for dead, so we ran with the crowd behind him and hooted all the way. We stopped for three piss breaks and four muffin snacks before we caught up with Rock, or where he was a few hours ago, according to a tramp we met. It was nightfall, and we'd been blown off.

'Can you remember the way back, cuz?' I asked Karim.

'Yeah. I ask Tramp.'

'Oh yeah, na la, it's somewhere over the rainbow and between the cottage on Lollipop Lane. Just go ahead and eat the chocolate door handles, smell the candy cotton chimney smoke, and wipe your ass on the grass. When you get back, you can hang with me if you like, but only if you like serving men good helper deeds and sleeping in the rain. Can you buy a bottle of bourbon on your travels?' asked Willy the Tramp.

'Did you catch all that, cuz?'

'Yeah, go back way you came.'

'Which is?'

'Back there. I'll ask the Tramp again.'

'Na fuck off, leave him be cuz. We'll camp under this tree until Rock comes back for us.'

But he didn't, and we had to fend off Willy the Tramp all night. Whenever we tried to get some sleep, he'd creep over and put his tongue in our ear, then use the excuse that he was looking for his pet flea. Karim believed him the first few times, or maybe six or seven, but after that, he copped a hammering from my Lebbo vocab chest of tricks. I gave it to him so hard he slept three metres away from us and put his dick away on command. I was really fucking influential when I had to be cuz, and when I put my foot down, mountains levelled.

'So where now?' asked Karim at daybreak.

'Back to the gym, I guess. We'll catch a taxi, cuz.'

'You money?'

'No, I gave it all to you, cuz. How much did the muffins and coffee cost?' Karim shook his head.

Just when we thought of asking Willy the Tramp for directions again, Shorty drove up in a fully restored Datsun 180B SSS. It was the model released directly after the 180B, so it wasn't quite as bad.

'Get in ye long grassers, we've got business.'

We piled in the back seat away from the midget maniac. He stank of smoke and had wet hair.

'Where were yer two last night? With Willy?'

'Ya know him cuz?'

'Yeah, he's my brother-in-law. C'mon, yes, or no? I can go back and check! In fact, I need to return his pet flea, but maybe later.'

'Swear to god, cuz. We were jamming with his pecker all night.'

'What?'

'Well, kinda cuz, you know what I mean, ay?'

Karim laughed and squeezed my leg.

'Alright, well me gyms no more. Little Credence,

Clearwater dead-shits burnt it to the ground. I want em on ice, boys. Can you find em?'

'We can go back and ask Willy?' I replied.

'Um, er, na it's ok. Anyway, we've got a fight to go to. If we can fill the stadium, then we'll have enough for the repairs. It's a $100 entry fee.'

'Huh? Who's worth that much, cuz?'

'I've got Rock fighting Imposter Poo, and it's gonna be sweet.'

'Don't you mean Kostya Tszyu, cuz?'

'Well, I think he's related. Who fucking cares, no one knows how to spell it anyway.'

'I do,' said Karim.

'Anyway, you boys will be takin' the money and selling water on the night. Yer understand? It'll be a fucking synch my little bubble bath friends. I'll give you a cut if you do well.'

'Yeah, I dunno cuz. We haven't been friends for long, and I'd consider this a personal favour, cuz. I'll need to confer with my right-hand Russian as well.'

'If yer say no, I'll take you back to Willy and lock

you three in the car for an hour. Your choice. You'll be sad and sore for a week after he's broken your water sack. Now, c'mon, I need an answer.'

'Well, I guess so, cuz. I don't want my jelly belly water sack broken now, do I, mate.'

'How about you, Karim?' asked Shorty.

'Already blown in a Russian prison.'

'Or was that payment for your mum's address in Perth?' I asked.

He looked at me and smiled.

'Alright then, it's settled. I'll drop yer both off. Go inside and man the water van. When people come in, take the $100 entrance fee and sell water at the same time. Ya got it?'

'Clear as fucking tadpole sperm, mate.'

'Karim?' asked Shorty.

'Clear as most beautiful noise in the world.'

'And what might that be, cuz?'

'Hammer and sickle banging together.'

When we reached the boxing stadium, Mickey stopped the car out front and gave us a ten-minute lecture about not fucking things up or else. I couldn't get a word in, cuz. We tried to slide out the back door feet first, but he kept on moving the car forward so we couldn't get out.

'Now yer a couple of fuckups, even an American hiding in a grassy knoll can see that. But I want ya to make me proud. Ya gotta stand up when things are a little slow, ya get it?'

'Yeah, I get it cuz, stand up for yourself mate, sit down, get up, good one. You're a real fucking genius, ay?'

Shorty smiled as if he'd won some kind of victory. But here's the deal, mate, if we didn't rake in at least 20 grand, the gym would be fucked, and I mean proper fucked.

'If ya don't rake in 20 grand, then we're all fucked, ya hear me, proper fucked!'

Jesus fuck me, the guy was both ESL and had ESP powers.

'Time to leave, Karim. Shorty, can you stop the car, please, mate? It's kinda hard to get out of a moving car.'

'Jump ya bastards, jump when you're ready. Show me how brave yer can be. Prove it, prove it to old Shorty, why? Because Shorty loves ya.'

This guy was sounding too much like a movie character who died in the movie and then died in real life again. His bullshit talk was contagious, mate, even I was starting to talk some shit.

Eventually, I talked the old fella around, but not before he did ten laps of the car park, bunny hopping the car like a gazelle fucking in springtime. Made a real scene, mate, I'm telling ya.

'Now make Shorty proud, ya Willy wankers, and don't try to tell me he didn't shag ya in the park. Willy gets everyone, everyone! Ya hear!'

I was really fucking confident we wouldn't meet that guy again, so confident that we planned to fuck the whole thing up and piss off back to Tex's joint. We were still in the good books for our bubble bath deal at the wharf, so a gym burnt to the ground and a whole boxing match gone to the dogs would surely be forgiven.

'Jesus mate, that Shorty's a psycho bastard, ay

Karim?'

'He loves Rock.'

'Yeah, I reckon you're right.'

'Need to do good, Costa Poo is fighting.'

'So, you're going for the Russian side? You sneaky fucking traitor. Rock's on our side, mate, he's our bread and butter, mate!'

'I cannot betray my Russian brother. It's like killing your own Mum.'

'So, it's Poo vs Rock ay? Ah well, our job is to get the money coming in and sell water, mate, got it?'

'Assie Assie oy!' said Karim in a sarcastic tone.

We checked out the water trailer and kicked the wheels a few times.

'Push the trailer close to the entrance, mate. Now, how are we gonna collect the money when they come in?' I asked Karim.

'Not know, water is my business. You do money.'

'Well, just wait here then and I'll get the water from

out back, mate. Make sure you don't let anyone in, you promise, cuz?'

'Sharpen my sickle and hope to live.'

By the time I arrived back with the water, the place was crawling with Russians. Karim got so excited that he agreed to 1700 IOUs.

'They good for it. I promise.'

'Aw yeah, you know him cuz?'

'Yeah, he Ramonov, good boy. I know him from today when he came in.'

'So, you don't have any door money?'

'They owe to me, they pay, it's the Russian way.'

Fifteen minutes into the fight, Costa Poo was losing mate, and no one would pay their IOUs. Shorty was too busy to come over and count the money, so we had time to talk with Karim's Russian mates.

'You, dog, pay. Hey you, big dog, maggot, shit paper,' screamed Karim.

'Hey Karim, I don't think that's the way to ask, mate. You need charm in this world, cuz. Here, let me do it.'

'You not Russian, they no talk to you.'

'Then they can listen, mate.'

'Good luck.'

'Hey, Russian dudes, KGB lad, black sea, and all that trash. You got the money you owe us, mother fuckers?'

'Hmm, that's good. Perfect Wog boy. Anyway, it's ok, I get them. They are from South Russia, me from the north. Me better at revenge. You go and watch the fight ringside for an hour. Let me handle it.'

'Are you sure, cuz?'

'Sure.'

'When I arrived at ringside, Shorty had split the scene, and Rock was crying in his corner, mate. Costa had beaten the living shit outta of the Italian gelato.'

'Rock, you gotta get in their mate, left-right, move like pepperoni on hot cheese. Say stuff to him, mate, yell at his pussy, I mean, at the pussy!' I screamed.

'I can't go on, yo, my head is aching ah! My back hurts, my teeth aren't clean!'

'Hey, what about that chick called Adrian? Do you

want her to come?'

'Never heard of her, go away, get Shorty back. Aghhhhh!'

I left the guy sitting on that pathetic footstool with his knees around his head. But we had bigger problems, as there were 1700 Russians surrounding our water van, all pissed as farts, wanting Karim's blood.

'Hey, what the fuck cuz, where did the booze come from?' I screamed on arrival.

'Fucking north Russian, he thinks his hammer and sickle better than ours, I kill!' said a foreign-looking Russian fella.

'How the fuck did you get so pissed?'

'The North Russian, he did something to water.'

I stepped into the water van and smelt piss on the floor. All the water bottles were opened and given away for free.

'What the fuck cuz?'

'They don't pay, so they pay another way,' said Karim.

'So why are they so pissed? On water?'

Karim pointed to his dick and made funny noises.

'Vodka in my blood, I have. Now in water.'

Well, I'll be fucked cuz. The sneaky Russian had so much Vodka in his bloodstream that he could serve his own alcoholic piss to the crowd. They were coming for him in droves, mate, yelling shit like, 'kill piss head and bash piss water boy' and all types of vile shit, mate.

Somehow, I managed to smuggle Karim out back when they turned on themselves. There were at least 1700 of those bastards that looked and talked the same, so I went around calling everyone Karim and they started throwing punches like piss-drunk Soviet sailors. I worked the crowd like a pizzeria pro, dodging and weaving until I copped one in the back of the head. I was punch drunk mate, but somehow, I made my way back to the drinks station where a couple of fellas were thirsty. I gave them two free bottles and a worn-out smile. They looked blurry mate, like fizzed-out crime figures on the TV.

'Hey you, dirty fuckers! Ya drinking Russian piss my man, I mean people of fuzzy decent. Hang on a minute, ya shit-lipped brass peanuts, you two dog fuckers look familiar.

Where ya from and where did ya come from?' I asked.

They muttered something in a foreign language, so I gave them two more bottles of piss water each. They seemed happy.

'I'm just gonna get the Karim boy from fuck knows where mate. You stay here and drink that free-living by-product of Russian excrement, and I'll be back for some foreign language instruction regarding your stupid accent. Are you happy with that, cuz?'

They laughed, but I don't know why, mate.

'Karum, Karum bum darling,' I said wandering aimlessly, 'where the fuck are ya buddy loy? Or should I say piss magic soda stream patent? I have a vision, Karum standing in the patent office, mate, with a bottle of Vodka, piss water, and all the paperwork to make a fortune, cuz. You could sell this piss water to the world, the world, I say, ahahhhh!'

I was talking to myself for the most part, mate, but I could see a figure squatting on the dunny in front of me. It could've been him or another vodka-poisoned lost soul. Didn't matter cuz as I was on fire without that piss ladened concoction. My punch-drunk status was legendary, mainly in my own mind, but that was enough for me!

It took me thirty minutes to drag Karim's sorry arse back to the van. He was passed out behind the ladies' toilets, totally smashed on his own piss cuz. God knows what he'd been up to behind the dunny, probably listening to all the groans and handbag zippers and how influencers on Instagram were dogs and sold themselves for money to Islamic oil merchants.

'Fuck world, fuck Poo! Did he win?' asked Karim with one eye open.

As my vision returned, I saw Tex standing at the end of the van, holding on for dear life. He'd drank three bottles, sharing the last one with Veronica. She was already trying to take his belt off.

'Ya fucking poisoned me! Don't deny it, ya, unconstitutional gun-holstered sons of bitches. Look what you've done to me, I can't even stand up!' said Tex.

Veronica was well into her handiwork by then, bobbing up and down like a ripe cherry in the wind. It made it kinda hard for Tex to talk properly, so I asked if he knew sign language.

'What?'

'Ah, it's ok cuz, I don't know it either. Don't feel bad, ay?'

'Fuck you, you, aghhh!'

'What happened, cuz? Are you alright, man?'

Veronica popped up from beneath the counter, wiping her lips.

'Oh yeah, Wog boy, he's just fine and dandy,' she replied.

'Well, I'll be blown by red lipstick on the fourth of July,' said Tex.

'Feel good, cuz?'

'No, not that ya rocky mountain timber wolf, you and that pervert Russian feeding us piss in a bottle. If that doesn't take the warthog at Christmas. I'm challenging you to a fight!'

'Aw yeah, Karim is keen, ain't ya buddy?'

He was still pissed on his own piss.

'Blurb man, star twinkle lipstick,' replied Karim, wobbling on his feet.

'So, it's set then, in the ring in ten minutes' time. You and me, Russian.'

'I'll be his trainer, ay cuz?'

'And I'll be Tex's,' said Veronica.

One hour later, we'd all made it over to the boxing ring. By then, everyone had left.

'You two talking racially divided varmint, I'm about to get evil with your insides. Are you ready?' asked Tex.

Karim chucked on the canvas.

'Fucking God damn unremorseful piss seller, I'm gonna wipe your face in that spew after I knock you out. I shit you not.'

'I shit you too cuz, right up ya brown dinger mate. Karim's, gonna take your 52 stars and kick them into the next universe. You'll be singing *Star Spangled Banner* looking through a microscope, cuz, ya hear?'

'Well, I'm lost for words.'

'Hey? Well fuck me with a red hat on saying *Make America Great Again*. Get him Karim before he opens his fucking mouth again. In fact, here's some duct tape. Plaster his mouth with it after he's down for the count.'

Karim started to play with his crotch.

'Hey, what's that in your pants, cuz? You better not use that, mate,' I said.

It was either his dick or an empty bottle, cuz. Of course, I'd seen his John Thomas a few times, in the public shower, so I knew it had to be a bottle.

'Ok, you dickheads, it's showtime,' said Veronica.

'Yeah, bad things are coming your way, cuz,' I shouted.

'Yeah, plenty of troubled times ahead, pizza base,' said Tex.

'Well, that's ok because I want trouble, mate.'

'Then you're gonna get trouble,' replied Veronica.

'When?'

Karim put his hand over my mouth and threw an empty vodka bottle at Tex. It hit him square between the eyes and shattered on impact.

'You dirty fucking Russian. He's the love of my life. Call an ambulance you dickhead,' screamed Veronica.

None of us had money for a phone call.

'Fucking hell Vince, here!'

She held up a one-dollar coin.

'Ok Karim, my beautiful cuz, you stay here, and I'll go outside.'

I snatched the one-dollar coin from Veronica and walked out onto the street. Karim came out afterward, and we blew the money on a discounted Mars Bar from the Ampol service station. Half an hour later, the deadly duo of Tex and Veronica came stumbling onto the street.

'Ok, Wog boy, you want it hard, you got it! You're going into the debt-collecting business, my low-life friends. Limmy will be here in thirty minutes to pick you up.'

'So, no hard feelings, cuz? Are we all good, Rambo?'

'Fuck off!'

A taxi pulled up and took their sorry asses away. Mate, what a pair of fuckups!

Chapter Six

Limmy dropped us off without saying a fucking word mate. He was either sick of us or didn't want anything to do with the new assignment. We tried to get the lowdown about what this new Bookie had to offer, but Limmy just kept waving his meat clever around saying 'bet fucked, bet fucked' or something.

I only knew that we were going to a bookie who ran the entire underground gambling scene in town. Well actually, I didn't know that, it's just that I've got a really fucking good imagination mate, like I can picture stuff in me head and it spews out onto the table. Mum used to call it bullshit, but I never agreed cuz. A good imagination really helps in life. After all cuz, look at where I am today?

We walked down the street not knowing where the fuck we were going.

'It Pom,' said Karim.

'It Pom?'

'It Pom.'

I looked up and saw a sign called *Pom's Laundromat*.

'Aw yeah cuz, of course, a laundromat, ay? Don't think this is our place, mate.'

'Nothing else street.'

And he was fucking right mate, every other building was abandoned with smashed up windows and shit splattered all over the pavement. Could've been dirt, but shit was more glamorous, rolls off the tongue a bit better ay?

We walked in and saw a punk broad counting change from a bag. There were whiteboards everywhere with numbers, brackets, and decimals, mate. It reminded me of high school when I was in the top maths class.

'Hey punky babe, what's all the maths shit splattered behind ya mate? Are ya thinking of going back to school cuz?'

She pulled out a knife and scratched her cheek.

'You're that fuckup couple Tex was on about the other night, ain't ya?'

'Yes,' replied Karim.

'Speak for your fucking self mate, I'm a high-grade Lebbo pedigree can of Chum cuz, spawned from the bosom of ancient fossil rocks and three hundred decibel sirens. I'm a fucking legend.'

'You look full of shit to me,' said a voice from behind us. Must have been *Pom*, the owner.

'He sneak up?'

'Too fucking right Russian, I'm the sneakiest bastard to ever sneak up on the dumbest fucks who ever lived. And in this case, you two. Pom is my name, son, now spill the beans.'

'Hey?'

'He means explain,' said the lady punk.

'About what?' I asked.

'About what the fuck you're doing here. Do I really need to ask?' said Pom.

'They're the fuckups Tex was on about at the bar the other night,' said the punk.

'Oh yes, the fuckups of the next century,'

'Yeah, I told 'em that,' said the punk.

'Hang on a four-foot dry well minute, no one is a

fuckup until proven so cuz. Me and my pedigree chum here have potential, otherwise Tex would not have sent us here to run your business, mate.'

'Oh, I see, is that how it is then? Run my business, will ya? Well, we'll fucking see about that won't we. Darling, did Granny Campbell pay up?'

'You got to be fucking kidding Pom, no one's got a dime outa her mate,' said the Punk.

'Well then, my pedigree major league fuckups, that's our play. Like James Bond at headquarters, your first assignment is to get the 100 dollars she owes me and bring it back to this very spot.'

'A granny cuz? Won't that be too easy, mate?'

'You can answer that question when you meet her. Now fuck off!'

We walked up the road and sat in a Lebbo fish and chip shop and talked for an hour about how we were going to upend the granny. Hopefully all her money would fall out of her camphor-ridden undies, cuz.

'So, what address?' asked Karim.

'Didn't you ask cuz?'

I shouldn't have asked him.

'Ok, you go back and get the address off the lady punk. I'll wait there and continue thinking.'

'Why.'

'Because I'm a thinker, can't you tell mate?'

Karim returned one hour later with jelly legs.

'Whatta ya been up to cuz? Did you shag the punk lady?'

'Why?'

'Well, you're all jelly like mate.'

'So maybe tired.'

'You weren't tired before, and it's just down the road.'

'So?'

'So, did you fucking shag her or not cuz?'

'Say different in Russia.'

'Well, no fucking shit mate. I'd never have guessed

that.'

He kept on zipping and unzipping his zipper, which was almost broken by now.

'So did you get the address?'

'Oops!'

The stupid fucking Russian was having such a good time, he forgot to get the granny's address. I was almost about to send him back when the punk lady walked by with lipstick smeared all over her face.

'Here, Karim, it's written in my best writing. Watch out, Granny's a fighter. See you next week, right, at the goth party on Main Street?'

'Ya, I love goth baby.'

She skipped down the street with her hand on her heart.

'Well fuck me KGB Casanova. You nailed her in the office?'

'Na, Russian love poem, always does good.'

'Love poems?'

'Yeah, from the secret halls of the Kremlin.'

'That's it, you just read her a love poem, mate?'

'What did I just say?'

'Ok, read it to me.'

'Na.'

'Fucking yes, or I'm leaving you at this Lebbo fish and chip shop that serves stale tabbouli salad.'

He prepared himself for a speech, like he'd just been elected to the head of the KGB.

'Hair spike, but you no dike, and if you like, I'll make you yike!'

Everyone in the shop laughed.

'That's fucking pathetic mate!'

'She doesn't think so.'

'Fucking women mate, they just need a little attention ay?'

Two hours later, we were at the front door of Granny Campbell's house. It was a nightmare trying to find the place ay Cuz. We'd caught three trains and a bus, going round in circles following grannies all over the place, mate. Karim reckoned every granny he saw was old dear Campbell, even though he'd never laid eyes on the old cow. He was fucking love drunk mate I'm telling ya?

'This looks like Perth apartment,' said Karim.

'It's not, and don't think that every granny you see from now on is your mum, ok? People get old, everyone gets old mate.'

'Include mum?'

'Yeah, including ya mum cuz, and mine. Don't you think I wanna wrap my arms around her black dress and help wax her legs mate? Not to mention fending off the hoards at the supermarket because she's bought all the eggplant on special.'

'You make up story.'

'Bullshit cuz, I remember when I was a young Lebbo on the north shore mate. It was the dream life I'm telling ya. Being teased at school then getting back at the can eaters with spit balls in the dunny, yelling at the pretty girls in Lebanese knowing they can't understand my sexual innuendo, and following the lady boys around with a big stick at recess.'

'You have lady boy back then?'

'Well, boys who looked like ladies, ya know, but not really.'

'Excuse me, dearies, are you looking for me?' said a granny at the door.

'I've been here for five minutes, didn't you notice me, dearies?'

'Aw yeah, course, cuz, can we come in?'

'No.'

'How come?'

'Because you haven't told me who you are or what you want?'

Karim laughed.

'Aw yeah mate, manners ay?'

Karim looked at me as if he wanted to take over.

'Look, lady granny cuz, I'm Vince and this is Karim.'

'So?' she replied, tapping the door with a walking stick.

'So, can we come in?'

'No.'

'Tell about Pom,' said Karim.

'Pom! You guys are from the debt agency?'

She quickly slammed the door.

'Cuz, you fucked up, how are we supposed to get into the broads house now mate?'

'Take look around back.'

We tiptoed out back and peered through an open window. She was holding a 1980's style TV in her arms. The thing was bigger than she was, with a one metre wide screen.

'Can we crawl through the window, cuz?' I asked Granny.

'No!'

'Aw come on mate, old cuzzina, we need to get this sorted.'

'I don't like anyone who wants to take my TV.'

We crawled through the window at the same time and got stuck. When I asked the old dear for help, she whacked us good and proper with a broomstick, five times each.

'There, that's for being fat assholes,'

'This old timer's going to be a hard case, cuz? You go in first,' I told Karim.

'Huh?'

'Yeah, you can't speak English properly, so you won't offend her.'

Karim got a few more whacks with the broom before he got in. I reckon the old duck felt sorry for him by that time.

'You're nice!' said Granny.

'So why hit?'

'I hit everyone, my dear, it's my exercise routine. Beats morning Pilates on the TV.'

'That why holding?'

'The TV?'

'Ye.'

'No, because it's all that I've got in the world, and

you two are going to take it, aren't you?'

'And why would we want a 1980s style TV with a one metre screen, cuz?' I asked with my head through the window.

'You shut up! I'm talking to this nice Russian fellow. Mind your manners. Your type always snob me at the supermarket, with ya funeral outfits and cash stuffed down ya nickers. You can cook, I'll give ya that though.'

'Lady grand cuz, can we please put race aside? We just want the 100 dollars you owe. Can ya pay up, mate? You got anything worth selling?'

'No!'

'Karim, can you go through all her drawers and check out her stuff?'

Karim walked around her bedroom opening and shutting cupboards whilst the old dear whacked him on the back with a broomstick. I managed to slip in the window at some stage and took a good look at the TV.

'Hey, lady, cuz, this might be worth something, ay?'

'Why do you think I was holding it you dumb shit?'

'Any cash stuffed down the back?'

'Oh yeah, do well when the things turned on, ay?'

Karim stood at her bedroom doorway playing with her old-style underwear that reeked of camphor.

'Maybe worth something?' he asked.

'You put them down! Very disrespectful! I'll give you the money, just stop with the fucking underwear!'

'Um, you swore cuz. Grannies aren't allowed to swear. At least my mum isn't.'

'I'll give you the money, wait here.'

She pushed Karim out of her bedroom and slammed the door closed. We waited for ten minutes at the kitchen table and made a cup of tea. I really liked those old-style cups with the blue and white patterns that made ya feel like you were in ancient Greece, mate.

'Here, take it and go have a bath,' she said.

Karim snatched the money without saying anything.

'Let's go,' said Karim.

'Oh good, you should've said that when you first

arrived. And you tell Pom that I'll be coming after him. He knows what for.'

We left in a hurry. The smell of camphor was killing us, mate.

'Give me the money, cuz,' I said as we got outside.

'Counted it already,' said Karim.

'Aw yeah, it's one bill mate. How hard is that?' I studied the note.

'You fucking dipshit! This is monopoly money.'

'Huh?'

'Ya know, the board game, mate, the square one that's got money and houses?'

'Yeah.'

'Bullshit cuz, you're just saying that. Do you know it or not.'

'Na.'

Five minutes later, we were out the back of Grannies again with our heads stuck in the window. She was sitting down drinking tea, pissing herself laughing cuz.

'Right, I'm getting tired of you old lady cuz, now

hand over the money.'

She slammed the window.

'Lady mate, little fella, can ya open up cuzzina?' I said, tapping on the window.

'Fuck off!'

'Karim, we're gonna need a plan, cuz. We can't go back to Pom's empty-handed, mate. We need that money or we're a whorehouse with a bad reputation. Can you think of anything?'

'Yep, watch me.'

He brought out a piece of paper from his back pocket and read it out loud.

'Please to be open well enough for us to keep employment for a long time to see our Mother and family.'

'What the fuck was that cuz?'

'I wrote when drinking tea. Look, she's crying.'

Granny walked over and opened the window.

'Oh, you poor, poor lad. You haven't seen your mamma in a long time. I understand, come give me a hug.'

Karim obliged but quickly backed off as the camphor burned his nose hairs.

'Ok, you got money then?'

She took and step back and slammed the window.

'So back where we started, cuz?'

'Hmmm. Smash window?'

'Ok, do it then mate.'

'She is crying again.'

'Just fucking do it.'

We looked around for a chair or a hammer, but there was only gravel, so we pegged around a hundred small stones through the window before it shattered. Noisy as hell mate, and took around an hour. By the time we'd cleared all the glass and jumped through, granny was locked in her bedroom again screaming stuff like, *up ya ass with broken glass* and *Nana Mouskourl hates yu guts*.

But when we picked up her TV and walked out the door, she followed us all the way outside.

'You can't take my TV, you half-cast vegemite hating outcasts, bring it back,' she said, running after us down the street.

'Walk to cash converters down the road, mate. They take anything cuz.'

The fucking TV weighed a tonne mate. We were doing the old lady a favour by taking it for her, but was she grateful, cuz? No fucking way. She hurled abuse at us until we got in the door, made a real scene at the front counter, mate.

When we plopped the thing on the counter, the attendant was already shaking his head.

'You can't bring that thing in here,' said the attendant.

'I know mate, you want me to take her outside?' I replied.

'It's my TV and I don't want to sell. I watch Sale of the Century every Sunday and knit my son a sweater.'

'You got a son, mate?'

'What did I just say? Now look, young man…'

'The name's converter,' he replied.

'Converter, that's really your name, cuz?'

'And why wouldn't it be?'

'Like cash converter mate?'

'First names, Andy, how may I help ya?'

'Well, mate, Pom wants his money, and this old lady owes. She's only got a drawer full of camphor-ridden underwear and a tea set that dates back to the dinosaurs mate, so we want a hundred bucks for this TV.'

'Well, let's see if we can help you. How old is the TV?'

'Well, I bought it on my honeymoon when my first love took my virginity and introduced me to marijuana.'

'And how long was that ago, ma'am?'

'I'm not sure of the date and time. I was stoned.'

Karim laughed.

'How old is the TV madam?'

'What? Can you speak up, young fella, I'm hard of hearing?'

'How old?'

'Well, it's hard to say. The years go by so fast and the memories, oh the dear loving memories, go by the wayside, and well, we make new ones, don't we?'

'Yes, we do, but that doesn't help us, now does it?'

Me and Karim had taken a seat by that time, talking about the fishing rods on the other side of the store.

'Do you have any children, dear? You look very capable of the old heave ho. I must admit, those strong legs must have a thrust about them? I can introduce you to one of my friends if you're keen?'

'Yeah, I'll keep that in mind.'

'So, you'll go out on a date with me then? You all heard it, you heard him say yes right, you two?'

'Jesus,' replied Karim.

The guy was pinching his nose at this stage and cracking his neck from one side to the other.

'So, do you want to sell it or not? We can put it in the antique section to see if it generates any interest. I can give you fifty dollars, ok?'

'Only if you go out on a date with me. I have a daughter, but she's in her sixties.'

This was getting better by the minute, cuz.

'Don't worry, young fella, I'm very experienced.

I've had a few kids and tried my best to have many more. I'll take you to a nice place on the outskirts of town. It's got nice bench seats and good lighting.'

'Actually, I'll need to square this with my boss.'

'Ow nice, where is he? Does he have any kids, and does he like it sideways?'

He flashed a fifty-dollar bill in our faces and escorted us outside.

Karim held up the money and Granny jumped for it. It wasn't long before she sprained her ankle and needed a piggyback.

'Your migration rejects ruined my date. He was about to say yes to the best thing that ever happened to him. You suck, both of you!'

'Could say the same to you,' replied Karim.

'Just shut up and take me home.'

'Not likely, grandman, you still owe fifty dollars cuz, you got it?'

'Oh yes, of course, just take me home and we can have a nice cup of tea and talk about it?'

'Like last time cuz, no fucking way.'

She slapped me.

'Keep her away from me, Karim. Make her walk, mate.'

'She ok leave alone.'

'Oh, thank you, young man. You deserve a kiss.'

What looked like a kiss on the cheek turned into a crusty game of hide and seek with her tongue. It seemed to go all the way into Karim's ear and out again. He'd need to go to hospital for sure and get some injections.

'She's not your mum Karim, you know that, mate?'

'Shut up.'

'Alright then, have ya little fantasy then, cuz. But remember, we've got a job to do, mate. This broad owes us $50, and we can't return to Pom without it.'

'Ay yes, Pom, such a nice little boy when he was young. I hand-stitched booties for the little tyke when he was three years old. I remember him well.'

'He's your son, cuz?'

'No, I stole him from a hospital!'

'I believe,' said Karim.

'Thank you, deary, you're the one with the brains, I see.'

'Na, he's not mate. Anyway, if he's your son, why is he trying to squeeze a hundred bucks out of ya? He can't just let it go, mate?'

'It's all history, dear. Water under the bridge, off a duck's back, through the canal, up the slope…'

Now, she was just shitting on mate. I didn't believe a fucking word she was saying. But I knew she was enjoying bobbing up and down on Karim's back, probably getting off on it, mate.

'Take her back to Pom?' asked Karim.

'Na mate, not without the money. Honey lass, you need to come up with another fifty dollars, then we'll take ya home.'

'I have another TV in the bedroom?'

'Na, I don't think so mate. How about jewellery or something? An old duck like you should have something to sell?'

Her ears pricked up, and she asked to be put down.

'Let's go over to that tree. It's nice and shady and we can have a rest,' she said with one hand on Karim's ass.

We didn't have a blanket or any refreshments, but I reckon that was lucky for Karim as she'd taken a shine to him, mate.

'Aw yes, deary,' she continued, 'When I was young, I was a dish…'

'Yeah, you told us that, mate.'

'Will you shut up and listen. Always these young dicks never listen.'

My dick twitched as if it wanted to get the fuck outa my pants and hide somewhere else.

'Yes, dearies, I was a dish, a real spunk in every regard. I had long legs, beautiful teeth and lips to die for.'

'So, you were a tart mate?'

'Yes, and so what? Tarts have more fun, so shut up.'

'I like tart,' replied Karim.

I gave him the evil eye. He didn't know what he was getting into, mate.

'Well, anyway, before I was so rudely interrupted by the Wog lad, I was a dish.'

'Ah fuck me mate,' I replied with my hands in the air.

'A beautiful woman who loved beautiful men, and then did lovely things to them when they weren't looking.'

'So that was your ploy, cuz? You jumped blokes when their backs were turned? That's really fucking good granny cuz?'

'Anyway, shut the fuck up. As I was saying…'

'Do you have fifty bucks or not, cuz I'm losing patience.'

'Yes, you Lebbo ignoramus! I have the money, but not in cash.'

'So, we need to go to Cash Converters again, mate?'

'No, we need to walk to the farthest cow paddock on the edge of the city and find an old oak tree, a beautiful tree that looks like something from a Robert Frost poem.'

'Ok, go on mate.'

'When we reach the beautiful tree, we look on the ground for a hidden gem that was buried long ago in terms of the utmost secrecy.'

'I see, mate.'

Karim was lost.

'It is there that a hidden gem is awaiting in the bosom of that tree, awaiting freedom,' she said, looking up to the sky.

'Ok, so where is this cow paddock?'

'Well, it's been a while, but I'm sure if we catch a taxi, then we can find it?'

'Are you sure, mate? Because if we don't, you will need to pay for taxi fare there and back, and we'll be back to square one, ya know that mate?'

'Let's not think ahead, dear. Come on, Karim, ya well-hung Russian spunk. Hail me down a taxi with your loving arms, tee-hee!'

We drove around until the meter hit $49. I wanted to save a dollar for a phone call in case we needed it.

'Here we are, just in time.'

'It's a vacant lot with houses on each side, and where is the tree, cuz?'

'Hmmm, strange. I swear there used to be a golden field here with trees that reached the sky. I used to read poetry here, you know, ran off my tongue like honey.'

'Yeah, and then?'

'And it was here that I shagged my lost love.'

Now she was just talking shit cuz.

'There is a ring under the tree.'

'Which isn't there now, mate?'

'Yes, seems so, but I remember where the tree was. It was like something out of a Robert…'

'Yeah, Robert Frost, I get it mate, woods on a snowy evening and all that crap! But I just have one question.'

'What's that, deary?'

'What the fuck are we doing here mate?'

'Looking for a lost treasure. An engagement ring that I threw at my love for the last time, lost forever under the earth of that tree.'

'Last time?' asked Karim.

'Yes, we had a turbulent relationship. The day after we got engaged, I threw the damn thing at him, and every day afterwards. You see, I wasn't sure if he was the one as he didn't believe in sex before marriage, and you know how I like the boom boom!'

She looked at Karim with lolling eyes mate.

'So, the guy wouldn't put out, and you made him feel bad about it, mate? That's really immature behaviour, cuz. You need to be more grown-up like me, mate. When I saw a Lebbo girl back in Lebbo land, I'd take off my shirt and sniff my armpits, right in front of her cuz. Then I'd do the Vince dance mate, bobbing from side to side like a peacock on heat. How about you, Karim?'

'Drunk on Vodka, then jump the lady.'

'Aw, you meat-filled holy communist you, Karim, you're my kind of seasoned sausage, my deary,' she said, looking him up and down.

We needed to find this ring, and fast.

'So how long are we talking about, mate?'

'Since when?'

'Since you lost the ring?'

'Oh good question, deary. Now let me see, I was born

on such and such and I was this age when he came along, then I left him and now I'm with you, and we are here.'

'Five years?' asked Karim.

'Spot on, you sneaky fucking Russian you. Let's put this plan on hold for a few hours whilst you and I deprive some grass of fresh air and sunlight.'

'No, we find the ring and sell it. Anyway, how the fuck did you get five years out of that equation? How old are you?'

'Eighty-five.'

'And you got engaged when?'

'I dunno.'

'Na, I can't do this mate. I'm calling Pom.'

'No, please, anything but that, he'll beat me, throw food scraps at me, and deprive me of affection!'

'Bullshit mate, he's your son. Unless you did something to him when he was a young fella, ay? Ok, we'll find out later, mate.'

It was a thirty-minute walk to the nearest public phone. Karim piggy backed the old dear halfway, who gave him the odd reach around, and put her feet down the back of his pants whenever she got the chance.

'Aw yeah Pom, we've got your Mum here with us cuz,' I said on the phone.

'And you're telling me this because?'

'She's your Mum, mate, be nice.'

'Look, mate, I sent you two to get $100 from a granny, and you can't even get that right. The fact that she's my mother has very little to do with it. I'm about money, that's it.'

'Ow, give me the phone, I know just what to say to the young fella,' said Granny.

I handed over the phone, but only after she tried to give Karim a dick pinch, you know, one of those quick grabs with an evil smile. She was nasty, mate, I'm telling ya.

'Ten minutes! With a car, now!'

'Ok Mum, where are ya? I'll pick you up, I promise. Where are ya, love?'

She handed back the phone.

'We'll catch a taxi to your place, mate, same

address?'

'Yeah, alright, and try and calm her down before she gets here. And I'm not letting the $100 go alight? Tell her that.'

'He says you'll still need to pay back the money, mate,' I said to Granny.

'So, he can fuck off! Hey there's a taxi. Hail it Russian boy!'

It took us an hour to get back to Poms, and when we got there, he was standing on the pavement.

'You disrespectful son of a bitch! Actually, I take that back, son of a…, well, son of a, nice lady! Get out here!' said Granny.

'Now, mum, there's no need for payback. It's just business, you understand?' said Pom.

She slapped him fair across the chops, mate.

'Get inside you little shit!'

We all piled into the office where the punk chick was manning the counter. She gave Karim a look, and Granny got jealous.

'OMG you fucked up little shit! You can't let a debt of $100 go for your old Mum?' said Granny.

'If you owe, you owe, that's what you taught me, did you not?'

She pondered.

'Well, I guess, but you know I don't have any money, and I lost my TV out of this whole deal. Now I can't watch Neighbours, Sale of the Century or Some Mothers Do Have em. You've ruined my life, even more than when you were born.'

Pom began to sob.

'Ow I'm sorry Pommy boy, I didn't mean that.'

'Yes, you fucking did?'

'Well, maybe a bit, but you were a bad seed from the beginning.'

'A seed you fucking planted ay? I want my $100.'

'I don't have it.'

'Well, I've got an idea then.'

'Ow fuck me with lightning bolts, you have an idea?' she replied.

'Yes! Do you remember the national granny arm wrestling competition I told you about last year?'

'No.'

'Ok, do you remember what you had for breakfast?'

'No!'

'Well, there ya go. Let me do the organising from now on, will ya?'

'No!'

'Ow fuck me!'

She slapped him again. This time with minimal effect, mate. The punk lady started laughing.

'Well, you're going to enter, and as you may be aware, you are the favourite to win.'

We all looked at her arms. We didn't notice before, but it was like she wore tights on her arms and stuffed newspaper underneath. A real fucking piece of work.

'It was the TV!' she said.

'What cuz?'

'The TV, that's how I got these arms, lifting it up and

down fifty times a day so some prick wouldn't come and pawn it! You see, you pricks ruined my life.'

'Ok, boys, take her away. Bring her to the comp at noon. Here's the address. Now, Mum, dear, your job is to reach the final, then blow it!'

'Will the other person be a man?'

'No, you perverted geriatric!'

She slapped him again.

'Right, now when you get to the final, you then lose on purpose.'

'But we'll lose money cuz?' I said.

'No again, you kebab marketeer, all my money goes on the other granny, and we get better odds. Mum, you get it right, this is what you taught me to do in the old days?'

'I don't remember, and where's my engagement ring?'

'No fucking way, not going there. Take her away, boys, and we'll see you all at the championships at noon. And by the way, if they ask you about accepting a handicap when you register, you say, no, got it?'

'Yeah cuz, loud and clear cuz. We're on it, mate.'

'And don't fuck this up.'

'Loud and clear, Pom mate, at the championships and no handicap. You gonna make the bet?'

'No, I'll just give you all the money so my beloved mum can spend it all on cotton candy at a hermaphrodite reunion. Whatta ya fucking think?'

She slapped him again.

'Don't you criticise abnormal people, dear. Everyone has a way of expressing their own individuality in this complex and ever-changing fucked up world.'

'What the fuck, did you read that in a cosmopolitan magazine?'

'Why?'

'Doesn't matter. Anyway, you know what to do, right? Now, all of you just fuck off?'

He got slapped again.

We were only ten minutes down the track, and the old dear wanted to take a dump.

'What, people your age still shit cuz? I thought you

folk only did it once a week in little tiny balls, like the sheep do?'

'Yep, that's about right. Now direct me to David Jones.'

'You shit there too cuz?'

'Yep, every time I walk in there a quarter pound of shit drops straight from my arse, so I need to make sure I'm ready deary.'

'Ready?'

'Yeah, ya know, ready to go.'

'And how can you do that if you're not in a toilet?'

'Well, I just shake around a little and make some room. I do this when going up the elevator, so no one sees me. If I jump around all the way up, I'm ready to go when I get to the top.'

'And the toilet is at the top of the escalators, right?'

'I can't remember. I'm hoping so.'

We gave in and let the old duck enter David Jones without an escort. After an hour, we had to go in and drag her out of the men's toilet.

'No, I identify as a man, but only when I take a dump. It's my right in this modern world.'

'May I ask why cuz?' I asked, pushing her out the front door of a toilet cubicle.

'It obvious, dear, look at the sign out front. It looks like me. I always wear pants! Not a single dress in my house! Look, it's me,' she said, pointing to the male figure sign in front of the toilets.

'So now you're a man, mate?'

'I was in the toilet, but now I'm a woman again.'

'But someone who can get Pom his money, right mate?'

'Yes, well, I've been thinking about that. Let's not worry about the ring deal in the park…'

'I thought you said it was a field, under a tree from a Robert Frost poem?'

'Yes, well, that was true, but I have a better idea now. Best not to live in the past, ay deary?'

'Na, the plan is set grandma, cuz. We're going to the national arm-wrestling contest. Don't you remember?'

'Yes, dear, but on the way, I need to lodge my Jobseeker form at Centrelink.'

'You're not on the age pension, mate?'

'Failed the assessment, my dear. It was my TV, you see, its vintage status, one of a kind. Worth a fortune!'

'The one you sold for $50 at Cash Converters?'

'Oh yes, is that dear old man coming to the tournament. I'd love to put my hand in his pocket, I would. Feel the cash up close, and maybe the snake that guards it, ay dearies?'

'You like Russian snake?'

'Karim, don't lead her on. She's just taken a sheep shit, so go easy on the old girl.'

'Ay yes, sympathy, I do like that I do, I do, yes indeed I do,' she said, clapping her hands together.

When we arrived at Centrelink, she said she needed to go back home and get her form.

'I need to go back, dearies! Perhaps we can have a cup of tea and I can show the pics of my beloved, the one I got engaged to and made love with under a beautiful fig tree.'

'The Robert Frost one?'

'Oh no, this was more like Tennyson and his field of daffodils.'

'No, cuz, I don't think so. You can just ask for another form when you get in there. Do you need us to come in with you, mate?'

'Yes, maybe, the security guards are very mean, they told off a senior citizen two weeks ago for taking a dump on the floor. The little balls of poo ran all the way down the corridor, quite the scene I must say!'

'Yeah, I bet, mate. Actually, I reckon we'll wait out here, mate.'

'As you wish!'

She toddled off like a merry duck mate.

'I think we go in,' said Karim.

'You think?'

'Yep.'

We followed her in, and quick smart lost her in the crowd, mate.

'Hey, you seen granny?' asked Karim to another granny.

'Granny Gilmore or Johnson? Or do you mean Sally from Lavington Avenue? Or Sally from downtown?'

'Campbell.'

'Oh yes, she's here, somewhere. What do you want her for, or is it too hard to explain?'

'Yes.'

'You look like someone I pulled from a boat once on Darling Harbour. Have you been in my country long?'

'Dunno.'

'Don't know or won't tell? You need to speak proper English in this country, young man, or you won't get very far, especially talking to people like me. I've been here my whole life, and I don't usually talk to foreigners. Are you Russian or Slovakian?

'Where is Campbell?'

'Hey, Russian dude, back of the line ya mobster freak!' said a voice from behind us.

'Hey, cuz mate, Centrelink is for all of us: wogs, freaks, mobsters, big mouths, anyone, mate. They hand out money like candy here, cuz. Wait ya fucking turn!'

A thick-set guy with tattoos on his shoulders moved towards us. He had a bikie jacket on with 1% logo on it.

'So, you got a 1% IQ mate?'

'Why?'

'Because it's written on your jacket you dumb fuck. Can't you see behind you, mate?'

'Not without a mirror.'

'Yeah, I suppose so mate, good comeback cuz. Now sit down and shut the fuck up mate, we're looking for granny Campbell.'

'Yeah, she's here?' he asked.

'Yeah mate, somewhere.'

'Right boys let's go. We'll come back tomorrow,' said the Bikie.

Ten blokes stood up and walked out. I counted up their IQs and stopped at 10, pretty impressive mate, especially at Centrelink.

'No, I want a new form and I want it now,' said Granny Campbell at the counter.

'Excuse me, madam, do you have extenuating

circumstances? You were paid last week, and payments are only issued once a fortnight,' said the front counter lady.

'You mean am I broke, have nothing, and suffering trauma?'

'Um, I'm afraid that simply doesn't quality you for extra consideration. You need to have evidence of sexual abuse, prisoner of war scars, tuberculosis, and a recent involuntary sex change. If we can tick all those boxes, then you get an immediate payment of $100,' said the bitch cuz from behind the counter.

'I see, well those fellas over there stole my TV and made me have sex with a cash conversion machine, then they bashed my son and made me attend a granny arm-wrestling convention, good enough?'

'And the sex change?'

'Well, I owe all that all to David Jones. Their toilets are so accommodating.'

The Centrelink lady took a hundred-dollar note and put it on the counter.

'Yes, cuzzina, you can pay back your debt.'

She ran out the front door and down the road. We

caught up to her ten seconds later, passed out on the grass with her legs twitching.

'Get the fuck up cuz, we know you're just playing dead.'

She didn't move.

'Pick her up, Karim.'

'By legs?'

'Yeah, ok, na better not. Lift up her skirt, nice and gentle, and get the hundred bucks out of her knickers.'

'You do.'

'Na, you mate! I'm the supervisor. Can't you see I'm important, mate?'

Karim flipped up her dress and saw the note lying flat under her bright white panties. The smell of camphor was killing us, mate.

'Fuck off!' she yelled as one leg came up on a right angle, missing Karim's head by a centimetre.

By this time, a crowd had gathered around us.

'It's ok cuz boys and cuszzinas, we're all from

Centrelink.' They nodded their heads and moved on.

'No, no don't go, they're trying to rape me. Help me please?'

The Centrelink front office cuzzina passed by as Granny was screaming.

'That's fantastic, do you know that rape victims qualify for an additional immediate payment of $25? Any rape victim with evidence of interference is right on top of our list. Here's the money, enjoy!'

'Jesus, cuz, these Centrelink dudes are pretty generous, ay Karim?' I said, stuffing the cash into my back pocket.

'Better than Russia; get Vodka ice-cream, middle eastern curry, and a cold shower. Australia, what a country!'

'Shit cuz, that's good English ay mate. That's the longest sentence I've heard you make. Hey, where's the granny?'

'Behind you.'

'I'm going back to Centrelink because I want to complain. You stole my $25 and I want it returned.'

'Na mate, we're going to the arm-wrestling contest, and if you don't win, you'll have to fork out that $100 in your knickers mate, got it?'

'You can put your hand down there for free, my boy, but if you take what's mine, I'll jam up on you, and you'll never touch anything with that hand again.'

I didn't want to think about it, mate, really.

'Ok, come, let's go,' said Karim.

Karim flung her over his shoulders.

'Oh Karim, you don't need to be so rough, my boy, but I do like a bit of the old rough and tumble, I do. So, are we going behind the shed or just here on the soft grass?'

'Tournament then home.'

'That's a fucking excellent plan cuz, let's do it!'

When we got to the tournament, there were wheelchair taxis everywhere, mate. The front door was lined with walking frames, and there was a bin full of water with a hundred or so dentures in it. The attendant gave it a stir now and then, sifting all the salami, sardines, and mango from the top with a small skimmer. It was fertilizer in the making, mate, fit for the best plants in the highest tower in Lebbo land. Smelt fucking awful though.

'Best not talk to anyone, dearies, they might get you distracted. Remember, we're here for a specific purpose.'

'No shit cuz.'

The phone rang at reception.

'Phone call for granny Campbell!' said the attendant.

Ten grannies raised their hands and went to the front counter.

'Who's it for?' asked one of them.

'Granny Campbell.'

Our granny grabbed the phone.

'Hello, this is Mrs. Campbell.'

'Hello, it's Pom.'

'Well, I won't hold that against you, deary. Apart from the Kiwis, you're our closest relatives.'

'No, Pom, you're son, you ignoramus!'

She slapped the phone.

'Remember what I told you at the office?'

'Oh yes, something about going somewhere, like this place. I believe I'm here.'

'Yes, you are, and what did I tell you about taking a handicap at the tournament?'

'Well, I think that's something you're born with, dear, not much I can do now.'

'No, not that kind of handicap. It's to do with being on par with others. It's a competition thing, love.'

'Oh yes, I remember, when I get to the final, I blow it.'

'Yes, that's right, my childbirth relative. And when I say you blow it, I do mean it!'

'Well, I've got the young and able Karim with me, so that shouldn't be a problem.'

'Now, ma, there's no need for perversion. There's a lot of money riding on this!'

She put down the phone.

'Um, Vince, how does the money thing work here again?' she asked.

'If you take the handicap, you might get an advantage and win. If you win, then Pom loses all his money.'

'Because?'

'Because he's going to put all his money on the other granny.'

She looked down at the ground and picked up some cash under her feet.

'Hang on dearies, look what I found. Can you count it for me, Karim?'

'Four, three, eight, ay?'

'Oh, for fuck's sake. Two … five hundred dollars. What about the extra hundred protecting your pink bits?' I asked.

She slapped me.

'Deserved,' said Karim.

'Yeah, I guess, but I reckon we need to return it, don't ya reckon Granny, cuz?'

'Oh yes, of course, honesty is most certainly the best policy, I totally agree, deary love.'

She paused for a minute.

'So where do we place the bets?'

'You're gonna bet on the other granny cuz?'

'Maybe.'

'How do you know you get to the final?' asked Karim.

'Final of what?' she asked.

'Well fuck me in a geriatric barnyard. I need some rest from all this shit mate. Karim. Let's get a coffee.'

Granny slapped me again, followed by the other nine grannies.

'Best not leave.'

'I need some respite, mate, perhaps a career funded by the NDIS or something?'

'That's me,' said Karim.

'Yeah, you fucking said it mate, now let's go.'

We left Granny Campbell with the other nine grannies and sat in the café area, where they served instant coffee and arrowroot biscuits. I could see the conniving geriatrics huddled in a group, like a washed-up rugby team doing a scrum re-enactment, mate. When they finally agreed on a plan, they jumped up and down, giggling like witches at a family reunion.

'What are you lot up to?' I asked on my return.

'We've heard what Karim's packing, and we want a piece!' said Granny Campbell, number six.

'Hey Karim mate, I think you'd better go and sit back at the café.'

'My Russian accent does it, mate.'

I addressed the Campbell babes.

'Now, Cuz ladies, can all the other nine Campbells please go back to your seats. I only need Pom's mum.'

'It's ok dearies, we'll catch up next time when Karim's minder isn't here, and we'll jump the Russian powerhouse in the gym mat storage area.'

'Yihah!' they all screamed, jumping up and down holding their crotches.

'Now, deary, take me to the bookie in the back area.'

'Why, mate?'

She slapped me.

'What was that for, mate?'

'It felt good, and I'm getting used to slapping people. Anyway, I'm your superior, so just take me!'

I was dubious, mate. She had six hundred dollars shoved down her pants, and the knowledge that Pom was going to fix the arm wrestle. Pom would only put down his cash when he was sure she'd reached the final mate, but she could then win and clean up if she put the dollars on herself. Sneaky fucking business this stuff, perfect for a sneaky fucking Russian sitting over in no man's land drinking cheap shit coffee. Takes the ones with brains to step up and bankroll the whole fucking city, ay cuz?

After half an hour, she came back and asked for help.

'Excuse me, deary, can you come over to the bookie and help me? He's asking some questions about handicap, but I don't have a disability. Unless being old classifies as one?'

'Well yeah, I'd agree with that. But keep it on the hush mate.'

Everyone in the room turned around and looked at me.

'So, what's this handicap, mate?' I asked the bookie.

'Well, if she's got things happening in her head or body, there are certain concessions.'

'Is this the handicap Pom was talking about Granny, cuz?'

'Who's that?'

'Ok. So, what does she have to do, mate?' I asked the bookie.

'I need to know all of her conditions so I can place her bet.'

I looked down and saw six hundred dollars in her hand.

'You betting the lot cuz?'

'No, I'm going to buy a coffee.'

'A six-hundred-dollar coffee?'

'Yeah.'

'Look, there are other people waiting. I need to know her handicap.'

'Just tell him what's wrong with you, cuz, apart from the obvious.' She slapped me again.

'Well, let me see. I've got Parkinson's disease, tuberculosis, thyroid dysfunction, retinal failure, renal failure, irritable bowel syndrome, ingrown toenails, false teeth, asthma, vaginal inactivity…'

'Hey, don't get dirty, old lady. I can't write that down.'

'Ok, sorry, love. Um, bipolar, depression, psychodrama association, convenient forgetfulness, misogamy, and … dry lips.'

'That's it?'

'Yeah.'

'Right, go and sit down.'

'Why do I have to sit?'

'I mean, go away.'

She slapped him.

'Can I put a bet on myself to win?' she asked.

'Ok, but you lose your money if you don't reach the final. You understand?'

'Of course. If I lose, I'll be rich and Mr. Wonka from Lollipop Lane will comfort me in my last moments.'

'Yeah, that's right. Hand over the money, lady.'

She threw the six hundred dollars in his face.

I went back and sat with Karim as I couldn't stand the old lady for another moment, cuz.

'What does she do at the bookie?'

'She laid a bet, mate, that's what. The guy wanted to know what was wrong with her.'

'Pom not like that.'

'Oh yeah, he did say no handicap, ay? But they all have handicaps, don't they?'

'Yeah.'

We sat there for two hours while granny after granny made a bet at the bookies. It seemed like the arm wrestling would never start, mate. Then, just as the line wore down, a fight broke out. It was on for old and older mate; eye gouging, frame belting, hickey slurps, and bad breath tongue wiggles were all on the cards, mate. Management had determined that none of the ladies were healthy enough to compete, and cancelled the comp, awarding the first prize winnings tour own granny Campbell number one on a default number of handicaps.

'Look dearies, I won on odds of 10:1 handicap status, my dearies. I'm $6000 richer!'

The other nine Campbells surrounded her and demanded a cut.

'Hand it out, Campbell, or we'll complain,' said one of the grannies.

'About what?'

'About being the real granny Campbell!'

'Did you write down your middle name, cuz?' I asked her.

'Oh, no, I don't have one. Our mothers weren't that sophisticated, love.'

And they were right. Noone could tell one bloody granny Campbell from the next, so she split the money ten ways and split.

'So how much?' asked Karim.

'Hang on, deary.'

'One, two … six hundred dollars!'

'Excuse me, Mrs. Campbell,' said a head official walking towards us. 'Did you find $500 dollars on the ground?'

'Um, no, I mean yes, I mean what?'

"Give it back dear, it's the right thing do.'

She went to slap him, but stopped.

'Yes, I guess deary.'

'Granny reached down into her underwear and pulled out the winnings.

'Here, $500, shove it up your ass ya stiff.'

'Why need, it been in your vagina,' joked Karim.

'Fuck mate, you made a joke, you Russian dog. I'm impressed cuz.'

The stiff took his five hundred dollars, and we were left with our original $100.

'Right, Mum, it's pay day,' said a familiar voice from behind us.

Pom snatched the remaining $100 and handcuffed his Mum's hands behind his back.

'Right, now get her in the car out front and tie her down with two seat belts. I'll let her go when we get back to her place.'

'Shit cuz, isn't that a bit rough mate. Tying up your own Mum?'

I shook my head in shock, mate, but I knew it was

the only way to get her home, cuz.

When we got back to her place, the cash converter guy was there with her old TV and flowers. When we released the old dear, she immediately grabbed the guy and dragged him inside.

'Right, so that's satisfied her for a while,' said Pom.

'Hell of a fucking assignment cuz?'

'Yeah, well, you two didn't make me any money, but you did recover the $100, which is why I sent you in the first place. I suppose you should be congratulated on a job well done.'

'Can you tell Tex?'

'You can tell him yourself. I'm dropping you off at the hospital.'

'Ay, is he sick cuz?'

'Na, not quite.'

Chapter Seven

From that moment on, I promised myself I'd never associate with another granny again; putting my own Mum aside, and maybe Karim's, if we could find her.

'I'm dropping you two off at emergency, Tex is around here somewhere doing business,' said Pom.

'Yeah, righto cuz. Look after that Mum of yours. Hope that converter guy is alright?'

'He'll be tied to the bed by his suspenders. But don't worry, they'll break eventually. She's got her TV back, so it'll be sale of the century, man about the house and some mothers do have em' in succession. All I wanted was my $100, really.'

All this effort on our behalf cuz but no cash coming our way. It was about skills, or so Tex said, but I reckon we were slaves to humanity, cuz.

'Here, go in and ask for *Brains*. Good luck dickheads.'

He did a burnout in the Emergency carpark and left black rubber marks all over the place. When we looked back, he'd been pulled over by the cops and was being strip-searched on the car bonnet.

'We're here for brains cuz,' I said to the Emergency front desk lady.

'I'm sorry, sir, we don't have that procedure available at the moment. Perhaps you could stick an external hard drive in the back of your head, like the Matrix, and learn Kung-fu in thirty seconds?'

'Aw, that was fucking brilliant lady cuz. You must have a god-damn IQ of 678, or were you being sarcastic?'

'I am simply responding to your answer, Mr. Cuz, is that your name?'

'Lombardi love. This is Karim.'

She licked her lips at the Russian.

'Oh, I so really wanted to know that,' she said with a cheeky smile.

Karim was getting good with the ladies, mate. A fucking babe magnet.

'So, I assume you're after *Brains* the mortician?'

'I dunno.'

'Then how do you expect me to know?'

'Yeah, that's it,' replied Karim.

She looked him over, licking her lips.

'Ok, go down the hall and take the next two left turns, then turn right, then left again. When you get to oncology, turn right again and go straight ahead until you see a large yellow sign with no writing on it.'

'Sorry, why is the sign there if it doesn't have anything written on it, mate?'

'It's brand new. As I was saying, when you get to the yellow sign, go to the desk and ask for Tom. He may be on holiday, so in that case ring the bell and wait for someone to come out.'

'Hold the fucking medical system mate, how the fuck are we supposed to remember that?'

'Should I be saying this to the Russian then?'

'How know Russian?' replied Karim.

'You stink of Vodka, and you look well hung, at least from where I'm standing.'

She now had one leg up on the counter, rubbing the

inside of her leg.

'Look, lady medical babe with an itch to shag Russians, I don't have time for this cuz, we need to find Brains.'

'I agree, you do!'

'Ok, we'll find them, I mean him, ourselves!'

'Do that,' she said with her middle finger in the air.

Seven hours later, we found the yellow signs, but they now had writing all over them, mate.

'Same ones?' asked Karim.

'Are we at the oncology department?'

'What that?'

'It's where everyone is decaying and falling apart on the floor cuz. There's blood and guts everywhere, mate, like a place where they slaughter cows or something.'

'Are you sure?'

'Yeah, I know everything cuz. Hey you, with the white gown on?'

Several people turned around.

'Ay, you with the white gown, and shoes on!'

They didn't move.

'Aw, fuck, where is Brains?'

One of them pointed to the end of the corridor.

'Fucking long one,' said Karim.

'Yeah, I know mate, the chicks always comment on it.'

We walked hand in hand down a dark corridor.

On the twenty-minute mark, we came across two people talking in the hallway. The bloke had a medical student pinned to the wall and his tongue in her ear. She had a sticky note pinned to his back saying *help*!

'Aw, lady student, babe, are you ok?'

The guy slowly turned around; enough time for the young babe to get away.

'Well, if it isn't my new students sent by Tex,' he said three inches from my face.

'Your brains?'

'Yes, and may I have your name? It's not Jehovah, is it?'

'The name if God?'

'Yes, well, I've often thought I'd meet him, you see, so I ask every new person I meet if they are him, or her. Is that strange?' he said with his head on a tilt.

'Ah, well, depends on what you mean…'

'By strange? I often like to finish people's sentences. It makes them feel valued, don't you think?'

'My name's Vince, he's Karim.'

'Ah yes, a Russian, how fitting!'

'How so, mate?'

'I don't know. Its just something clever to say to an ESL person. They never talk back, you see, how delightful. But they still feel pain, I assume, and their screams, oh their screams, they do enchant me, I must say.'

For the very first time, Karim looked scared, mate. I was fucking scared.

'So, what's your job here, mate?'

He turned his head and looked away. He didn't move very fast, and he had an eerie sense of death about him mate.

'Oh, goody, goody, I do like games. Well, I could always tell you I guess, but that just wouldn't be sporting.

Let's walk down to the morgue and find out now, shall we?'

He walked out front taking his hat on and off, practicing his curtsey for whatever fucking reason.

'He's strange,' whispered Karim.

'Aw ya fucking think mate.'

'Define strange for me, will you. Oh, I am intrigued to know. Is it when someone is different from the status quo, or does something better or substandard to you? I practice my courtesy, not only at work but at home too. It makes me feel, well, different.'

'Yeah, ok, where's Tex mate?'

'Well, he was with me, so now he must be somewhere else. But I do have instructions to teach you all there is to know about the Mortuary business. Are you two considering a career change? Would you like to work for me, perhaps?'

'Career change, yeah, you could say that mate. I'm about gaining skills to make my Mum proud when I get home.'

'And you, Russian?'

'Same, when I find Mum.'

'So, you feel unloved, I assume? Nothing a good, long stint in a mortuary won't fix. Plenty of personality where I work. You just need a little imagination.'

We came to another hallway where the lights flickered, and water dripped from the ceiling.

'Not much further, my new experiments. Just make sure you keep your mouth shut.'

'No more talking, mate?'

'No, it's the flies. You don't want to catch one in your mouth after it's been checking out Mr. Becker, who was beheaded in a front-end crash with a semi-trailer, do you?'

'You don't keep em locked up mate?'

'Flies get into places where they aren't allowed. It's their nature, you see.'

'Oh, shit mate, I can't go five minutes without talking cuz, it's undemocratic, it's…' I began to cough my guts up.

'It's a fly in your talkative mouth, my juvenile friend. Now cough it up and keep following me. Give him a hit on the back, Russian, I'm sure that will help.'

'Glad!'

Whack!

'Work?' asked Karim.

'Na. I swallowed the fucker. Ah well, not the first one I've eaten, ay?'

'Yes, and a little of Mr. Becker is now inside you. How do you feel?'

'Ah, you're just fucking with me cuz. This is a test of character, mate. I can tell.'

When we got into the mortuary, the light had improved. There were draws everywhere: big ones, small ones, and sealed ones with special notes all over them. I tried to read the writing, but it was too small with all the wrong grammar.

'Now get a feel for the place, my Neanderthalic friends. Smell the air around you, feel the slime on the tables, see the flickering lights and how they absorb the energy from the dead.'

'Can we have a look at a corpse mate?'

'All in good time my half crescent moon colleague. As the black wiry hair will eventually fall from your mother's legs, so does the life of these unwilling participants.'

'Sorry, can you repeat that, mate? What do you do here?'

'I look after the dead, my boy. Make sure they don't get too smelly, and let families in to identify what they fear the most.'

'That's sick mate.'

'No, it's an art form, my boy. No different than a sculpture or a painter. I bring life into those who've had it taken from them. I am, as some would say, the master artist.'

'You can bring them back to life, mate?'

'No, you idiot, I was being philosophical. Now, wait here, I need to pick up some chemicals from bay 23. Just look, and don't touch anything else, and especially don't open any of the drawers. Do I need to lock them?'

'Ah, na cuz, all good mate. We can be trusted, ay Karim.'

'Yeh,'

'Very well, I'll be back in thirty minutes. Play some classical music if you like, get a feel for the afterlife as if it were your very salvation.'

Jesus, mate, what was Tex on about? What skills could I learn from this bloke except how to talk like a raving psycho and keep dead people company? I mean, do they even know that someone is here watching them?

'Hey Karim, let's open a drawer and take a snazz?'

'Ye said no.'

'Yeah, I know. But it's because he said no, that's why I want to. Isn't that the way it works, mate?'

'No.'

'Ah, don't be a chicken shit. What are mortuaries like in Russia?'

'Hole in ground, dropped feet first with one inch bottle of Vodka for the afterlife.'

'You don't keep them in a place for burial later, mate?'

'Sometimes.'

'How do you preserve them mate?'

Karim smiled.

'Aw fuck me cuz, no, don't tell me, na please no mate.'

'Yeah, we fill with Vodka. Make them healthy and alive again. Open up the drawer, I show.'

When I pulled out the first draw, I saw an old lady dressed in black with piano legs, cuz. It looked a lot like my Mum, so I rolled her back in and went for the next one. Fingers crossed it was just another Lebbo Mummy that'd eaten too much rotten pesto pasta.

The next one had a yellow sticker on his toe.

'Smith, good name for experiment. I show how to embalm Russian style.' said Karim.

He rolled over this hose like machine with a big needle on it and filled the glass cylinder with Vodka, mate. I think he kept it all down his pants. Maybe that's why the chicks thought he had a big dick cuz.

'Now, the artery is between legs, and fill. He may come alive, not sure.'

'Hey mate, that wasn't the deal cuz? You said, well, you said … sorry, what did you say?'

'I say come alive.'

'Ok, so what if he does, mate?'

'He acts like a psycho KGB reject.'

'Why reject?'

'If reject by the KGB, it great dishonor, like no ginger in your tabouleh salad.'

'Really, Tabouleh salad has ginger in it?'

'You know my mean?'

'Na, not really, but that's ok. Now I know to put ginger in the Tabbouleh salad, mate. That would've been embarrassing when I got home, ay cuz?'

He jammed the pipe up the guy's ass and let go with the vodka.

'Cuz! You said in his major artery inside the leg. Where did the ass bit come from?'

'Ass bit?'

'You shoved it up his ass mate.'

'So, I missed. You going have baby?'

'Where did you learn that shit cuz? You been watching TV between our little adventures? You need to talk to me before having access to education, mate. I'm your master cuz mate, ya hear?'

'Shut up.'

Karim continued to pump vodka up the poor guy's ass; slow, then fast until he got a good rhythm going mate. Even I was starting to get excited.

'He twitched.'

'Are you sure?'

'No, me keep pumping.'

'Na he's had enough cuz. It's only supposed to keep him from rotting away, mate.'

'Ok, I mix with formaldehyde.'

'You mean that mean shit chemical that cleans drains when rats shit in them?'

'I dunno. Stand back, it smells.'

He mixed the formaldehyde with the vodka and kept

pumping away.

'He twitch?'

'Ok Karim, that's enough mate. He's as white as a teenager caught wanking by his mum.'

'More.'

'Na stop mate.'

All of a sudden, Mr. Smith opened his eyes and began yelling profanities, like 'get that fucking wet dog outa my house' and 'it's your turn to be on top bitch, so don't be lazy.'

'Put pillow on face.'

'What, kill him again, mate?'

'Yeah.'

'What do I look like, a seven-foot American Indian suffocating a Vego after a lobotomy?'

'Yes, you do.'

I took the pillow and jammed it over the guy's face. He kept muttering stuff underneath like 'don't you dare discontinue making fantails, you bastards' and 'why the hell was the milkman delivering at 3 am this morning?' Sounded like the guy had marriage problems when he was alive and kicking, cuz.

'Let him go cuz?'

'Are you crazy? He kill everyone.'

'He's getting hard to control, mate. What do I do?'

'Ok, let go, I'll smack him back head if he tries to run away.'

Mr. Smith jumped off the table and landed in the sprinter starting position. He rose and pumped his chest out before opening his eyes.

'Ay cuz, are you ok mate?'

'Your attitude, give it to me,' he said in a Bulgarian accent. 'Really, you want my attitude? How long have you known me, cuz?'

'Um, your attitude, give it to me,' he said again.

'No, I don't think so. Do people in Bulgaria speak English?'

He looked confused.

'I'll be smack,' he said.

'Hey?'

'I'll be smack.'

'Really, you want your ass smacked? After all the vodka we've just pumped up your ass, you still want it smacked? Man, you're a fucking saddest mate.'

The guy ran off using a textbook Jessie James technique. He worked up a speed down the hallway and we lost him pretty quick.

'Why are you still here?' asked Karim.

'Why are you, mate? He's closer to your race than mine, cuz. Aw shit, it's Cannibal Lecture, he's returned.'

'Oh, excuse me, liberators of the modern world, don't let me disturb your Frankenstein-like behaviour. Are you planning on finding dear Mr. Smith before the vodka wears off?'

'I know nothing,' said Karim.

'Ah, I see, well it's a well-known trick in Russia to embalm a client using 90% proof vodka, it's almost as good as formaldehyde, you know?'

'I see,' replied Karim.

'Well, I do hope you're going to find the dear man. I

assume the Vodka has worn off by now and he's lying on the floor down the corridor. How much did you pump into his main artery?'

'Um, lots, but up bum,' said Karim.

'You pumped Vodka up the arse of one of my clients? Hang your head in shame you cold war, hairy assed shemale. You have disrespected my second home, now go find him before he gets a job as a doctor.'

We ran down the corridor like two drunk Sodomisers and found Smith at the end, flopped on his back mate.

'Give more vodka.'

'Yeah, like hell mate, Mr. Chianti and his Father Beans are close behind us, cuz. We're gonna have to drag the lug back down the corridor.'

'Whatever you do, my newly appointed death watchers, don't drag or you'll tear him apart,' said Brains from down the hallway.

'Huh, what the fuck is he talking about mate?'

'Dunno.'

We dragged the poor fellow, and halfway down the

hall, he suddenly got lighter. We couldn't see very well, and by the time we got into the light, we had a leg each and no torso. Brains came charging at us with a pen in his mouth.

'What did I just say?'

'Something about brag, mate?'

'No, I said don't drag him or you'll tear him apart, are you deaf? How am I supposed to explain this to the mortuary director at the funeral home? He died of a heart attack, not in a car accident.'

'Sorry cuz.'

'Well, there's no way around it now, my half-bred apprentices. One of you will have to pass off as Mr. Smith at the *South Side* funeral home tomorrow. It's a cremation ceremony, so you'll be in the box for the viewing, then we'll switch the body just before the cremation.'

'He's a thick set guy, ay cuz?'

'That he is Master Lombardi, as thick set as you can get.'

'And he's Bulgarian?'

'Spot on.'

We both looked at Karim.

'No.'

'Fucking yes! You pumped vodka up his ass when I said no, so it's you that's lying in that coffin tomorrow, got it?'

There was a long silence.

'And if not remember to switch the body before cremating?'

'Then I don't remember. It'll teach you to listen to people who speak perfect English, ay?'

'I speak perfect English and you didn't listen to me?' said Brains.

'Look, it's just a way to get power over the ESL community, ya know, like power and control and all that stuff mate.'

'I see. Well, be at this address at noon tomorrow. The viewing is at 1 pm.'

'So, we can go, mate?'

'Well yes, ok, but you are minus a torso, and a head down the hall. I think you'd better return it all and place it in the drawer, don't you? Oh, and mop up all the shit and vodka that's spilled out of the old boy's ass. It looks like a fine texture indeed. I'm off home, it's my wedding anniversary, you see, and I'm preparing a special meal of lamb's brains in Benedictine. You should pop by sometime?'

'Yeah sure,' replied Karim.

I think he was serious.

The next day at *South Side* Funeral Home.

'Don't fucking knock that loud Karim,' I said.

'It funeral home. Who wakes up?'

'Look, this is a really fucking sensitive situation cuz. We've got to take care of this problem before Tex finds out, mate. He'll be really pissed cuz.'

'First go back and mop hospital?'

'Hey? You didn't clean up all the vodka and shit before you left last night? I thought you did it when I went to take a leak, cuz?'

'Oh yeah, I mop shit all the way in hallway when you take ten second piss.'

'Well, you didn't say anything, mate. I thought you'd finished.'

'Who's making all that racket?' said a man on the

other side of the door.

'Ah, it's just us mate, Brains sent us over cuz.'

A midget with moppy dark hair opened the door.

'Boss, it's the dame boss, the dame!'

'Sorry, dame, what dame mate?'

'Oh, please do excuse my assistant,' said a tall man who appeared out of nowhere, 'he can't speak much English. We used to live on an Island that bore fruit from the heavens, you know, and now, we bring the dead to their final resting place. A fitting end to our careers. Forgive me, I am Cedric, and this is Ponto. We are the directors of *South Side* funeral homes. I believe you are delivering Mr. Smith this afternoon?'

'Ah yeah, bits and pieces, cuz. Did Brains fill you in?'

'I believe he was busy this morning mopping the mortuary corridors. Some kind of water leak, I believe, made a horrible mess, I heard.'

'Aw yeah, the vodka shit. That'll take him a while, ay?'

'Excuse me, vodka shit?' asked Cedric shaking his head.

'Well, maybe Mr. Smith is on his way by courier. FedEx will transport anything cuz.'

'I think you two had better come inside and explain.'

The midget served iced tea and rumballs on a polka dot tray. When he came into the room, we only saw the top of his head, and when he popped up between our legs to say his 'dame' thing, we cringed at the thought of him burying his head into our crotch and having to pull him away. He was like a miniature bull terroir that wanted pussy at all costs mate.

'So, you say Mr. Smith will be delivered after the family viewing?'

'Yeah, that's right cuz. Good plan hey?'

'Yes, excellent plan, my rocky road friend. Just one question; who will be in the coffin?'

'Aw yeah mate, haven't got to that part mate. Enjoying the tea and rum balls, mate. Really good ay cuz. So, where do you get the chocolate for these, mate, and what kind of tea is this? I'm really interested.'

'The chocolate is from Coles and the tea is from the same place. Now, my young friend, back to Mr. Smith, where is he now?'

'He's at the morgue mate, with Brains the lecturer mopping up vodka shit.'

'Yes, and Brains will deliver him, after the viewing?'

'Spot on cuz, you're a fucking genius!'

'The dame boss, the dame!'

'Oh, please be quiet, Ponto, I'll make the call to *Asian sweethearts* in a minute. You'll be happy, I assure you.'

The little fella ran into his room with his hand on his dick.

'Now, back to the original question.'

'What's my name cuz?'

'No, not that far back.'

'Who in casket during viewing?' asked Karim.

'Yes, thank you, my Rocky Balboa adversary. That

was my question.'

'Karim mate.'

Cedric looked at Karim and sized him up.

'Mr Smith is Bulgarian.'

'Yeah, so what cuz?'

'Well, he is Russian. Don't you think the family will notice, especially after knowing the deceased for 58 years?'

'That's not long, mate.'

'Oh really?'

'Well, not in historical terms anyway.'

Cedric stuffed a rum ball into his mouth and chewed slowly.

'Now, look, I'm sure we can pull this off cuz. Just use a little eye shadow and cut his hair all nice like … and put some pancake on him cuz.'

'And if they realize he's not their dearly departed?'

'We'll push the fire alarm.'

Karim laughed.

'By the time everyone has come back after standing out in the hot sun for an hour, the coffin will be gone and service over.'

'Hmm.'

'Good idea cuz?'

'No, but it's better than no idea, I guess. Karim, are you sure you can lie there for an hour and not move?' asked Cedric.

'No.'

'Look, Karim, you can do it, mate. Just fall asleep and think of one of those Russian ballerinas sitting on your face. You're also allowed to fart, as dead people still do that.'

'Not in my funeral home. I put cork screws up the arse. Any objections, Karim?'

'Yeah, he'll be right. He's been in the KGB, mate. They do all sorts of perverted shit mate.'

An hour later, Mr. Smith was out back in the crematorium, and Karim was in his coffin all dolled up to the max, cuz. We did practice runs of people walking by, even kissing him on the forehead a few times and whispering sweet things in his ear. He was pretty good mostly, but when Ponto jumped into his coffin with his 'dame' speech and licked the inside of his nostrils, the old Russian lost his shit and chased the little fella around the room.

The coffin tipped over, and we were back to square one. It was lucky we still had five minutes up our sleeves, and the guests were in the waiting room, mate. Cedric quickly called the Asian pleasure house and got the little fella a trafficked teenager, then locked the pair in a room for a few hours. We were set to go cuz.

'Welcome guests and uninvited others,' said Cedric to the crowd.

'We are gathered here to pay homage to the only Mr. Smith in the phone book. He is well known in famous movies where he duplicates himself and fights the one and only Neo Dick in the streets of New York. But that's in his dreams, of course, where he is at this moment. In regular life, he was downright boring, as you all are. When I look around this room, I see punch cards that fit nicely into an annoying machine that makes an even more annoying sound. Smith was once like you, but now he is dead, free from the bullshit, the never-ending dinner engagements where no one likes each other. We are all prisoners to this way of life, one that Mr. Smith endured for 50 odd years. He was both faithful and an adulterer, a statesman, and yet ignorant. He was everyone and no one. He was simply, Mr. Smith.'

Cedric got a standing ovation, mate. Then Karim farted and they all fucked off out the front door.

'Ok then, turn the oven on, Ponto, let's get this over with. Ponto?' asked Cedric.

He was still locked in his room with his faithful handmaid.

'Ok, looks like I had better do it. You two need to go back to the hospital. Brains wants to talk with you about the Vodka zombie, or something?'

'Shit mate, ok Karim get outa the coffin mate, we're going back to the hospital.'

'Me get paid?'

'No, because I'm not getting paid. This funeral was a farce, a farce I say, but quite good fun, wouldn't you say?' replied Cedric.

'Yeah, cuz, a ripper deal mate.'

'So goodbye, my foreign friends. I hope you survive Brian's anger management crusade, and I bid you farewell. Now piss off.'

When we got back to the hospital the bitch chick at the front counter was still there. It's as if she had 24 hour shifts back-to-back just to piss everyone off cuz. She looked worn to the max mate, with streaky marks all the way down her cheeks, and sticky hair like it hadn't been washed for a month.

'Hey bitch cuz, you still here mate. You been shagging the customer's mate?'

'Of course not, why do you ask?' she said, straightening her dress with both hands.

'Only joking, love, actually you look great, well, no, you don't. Do you have any time off?'

She was eyeing off the Russian again.

'Brains is looking for you two. He was here until 4 am last night mopping up vodka shit.'

'Oh yeah, we can handle that bloke, ay, he's nice once you get to know him, cuz.'

'So, how well do you know him?'

'Not at all, but it's something you say when you

don't know how things will turn out, mate.'

'So, you're a bullshit artist?'

'Yes,' replied Karim.

'Oh, I like your Russian. Do you have time for a cup of coffee?'

'Na mate, I think you've had enough trim for one day. It looks as if you've been through the entire hospital in that laundry cupboard, patients and all, mate.'

'Yeah, so?'

'Yeah, so where is Brains?'

'Standing behind you.'

He was wearing a ski mask.

'Hello, my evasive menial task avoiders. Did you miss me?'

'Ah, sorry mate, I can't hear you very well with that mask on. Can you repeat that, mate?'

He kept talking about revenge, war, and love. It was all muffled and shit talk cuz.

'Look cannibal cuz, sorry about the vodka shit ok, Karim did his best to get everything under control, but you're not helping with this ski mask rant mate, alright?'

He pulled out a pool noodle from his pants and chased us around the hospital.

'What, that was a pool noodle? All this time, you phony prick. No wonder you never took it out of your pants in the cleaning cupboard,' yelled the front office lady.

'Hey mate, easy with the pool noodle cuz, that's a lifesaving device, not a weapon.'

We ran through the many halls and corridors of the hospital, screaming and yelling profanities at Brains. He took a few swings at us, but he missed luckily. Real close one, mate.

When security finally arrived, Brains had us cornered in the geriatric ward. The old fellas were placing bets on who'd come out on top, and the nurses were cheering on Brains, as they had to empty all the mop buckets late last night.

'Kill 'em, Brains, give 'em the old flotation whammo,' said an elderly man.

Just as Brains was at the top of his backswing, security injected him with something from behind.

'Yeah, there ya go cuz, you deserved that ay?'

We were next.

I woke up with the biggest fucking hangover and a crabby nurse looking into my face.

'You are not allowed to leave this vicinity, do you hear? I am Ms. Clock, and I run this psychiatric facility with an iron fist. Everything on time, that's what I'm about!'

'Is that's why your last name is Cock mate?'

'I said Clock, and if you can forget that, perhaps there are other things you may forget. Nothing a lobotomy won't fix, eh, Steven?'

'Yes, Nurse Clock, your power is absolute.'

'Thank you, Steven, you make me feel all wiggly when you say that.'

'Yes, nurse Clock,'

'Hang on a tick, how about Brains? Why isn't he in the shit?' I asked.

'He is an employee of the hospital. He was simply doing his job. A pool noodle is not classified as a controlled weapon, so he's free. But, injecting corpses with vodka in the anal region most certainly is a crime. I reported this to the authorities, but they laughed at me, so I convinced them to hand you over to me.'

'You?' I asked.

'Yes, my public siren-loving friend, you and your mobster mate are mine.'

'You mean Clock sex slaves?'

She pulled out a cattle prod and stuck it up my shorts.

'That's as good as it gets, my friend.'

'Remarkable discipline, Ms. Clock. Well done.'

'Thank you, Steven, very kind.'

I was in pain, mate, my gonads were throbbing like an imploded submarine chasing after DiCaprio's sunken love boat.

'When you're able, meet us all in the recreation room down the hall. I believe Karim has already taken to ping pong with our resident hang-sengman. He's an ex-Chinese champion.'

I stood up and my legs failed me, or perhaps it was my balls. I felt like I'd never screw again, or perhaps I was already thinking that after I met Mrs. Clock mate. Anyway, I could hear a right fucking commotion down the hall, so I leant against the wall and made my way down.

'Limmy, what are you doing here, mate? I thought you went on a bubble bath job?'

He didn't respond. He just kept playing table tennis.

'Your hang-sen-man?' I asked.

'Ping on ball, lobotomy dim sim.'

'Oh no mate, you've had a lobotomy cuz? Fuck, you'll never be able to make a proper sentence mate. Are you ok?'

'Clock cock dick, hefty bitch.'

'Fucking oath mate, you said it. But try and remember your name, mate. It's Limmy, remember, the meat cleaving world warrior?'

'Pin head dick.'

'Ah, it's alright mate. I'll help ya later.'

As I leaned against the table, I could see characters from all walks of life, mate. Most people were laughing about stupid shit that didn't mean anything, or wanted to laugh but couldn't remember how. Head dick Ms. Clock was always watching in the background mate, the eye of all eyes looking, scanning, scheming for a revolutionary to take over and do her out of a job cuz. I was the only one there with half a brain and a decent imagination, so I worked the crowd and got myself into the know, mate.

'Hey dickhead, what's wrong with you mate?'

'There's nothing wrong with me. I'm perfectly fine. I have a job and kids, and a wealth of experience to offer the world. I'm being released, you know, sometime next week, or perhaps today. I'm a scientist, no an astronaut, and a teacher. Can you speak English?'

I moved on to the next one.

'Willpower, that's what the world needs, willpower. The ability to get things done and move mankind into action, like a plan of how to make America great again without wearing a stupid red hat and giving car makers key roles in the government.'

I moved on to the next one.

'People are strange in this place, little fella. I talk decent, but they don't talk decent back. It's not me, you see, it's them, and those little minds that keep arguing against my logic. I am smart, you know, but I don't like to show that side to people. I keep to my bedroom with my stuffed toys and Tinkerbell mobiles, hanging from my ceiling. It helps me sleep.'

'Limmy! Can you please come over and talk to me, please!!!'

'Dum fuck love mum, ping pong me, and who Limmy?'

'Karim, come here!'

He walked over looking pissed. I'd interrupted his game of table tennis.

'Ha?'

'I need someone to talk to.'

'Why?'

'Because I'm lonely cuz. This place is full of weirdoes.'

'It mental asylum.'

'Yeah, I know, but I don't like it here.'

'So?'

'Ok then, fuck off, I'll sit here by myself.'

Everywhere I tried to sit was taken by someone else. Each chair had someone else's name on it, and I got hassled when I tried to sit.

'That's my chair you're stealing, you no good bastard. Don't you have any sense of personal property? I will advise Ms. Clock that a full lobotomy is warranted if you sit there again. And by the way, you shit me!'

I eventually made my way to the corner of the room and sat with my head between my knees.

'You Vince, Vince Lombardi?' asked a familiar voice. 'It's me, Steven, Ms. Clock's right cock man, I mean, right hand man. Do you remember me?'

'Vaguely, mate.'

'You have been identified as a class one troublemaker by Ms. Clock and scheduled for a lobotomy at 8 am tomorrow morning. Do you have a preferred time?'

'You mean other than 8 am?'

'Yes.'

'Ok, midnight.'

'I'm sorry, Mr. Lombardi, 8am is the only timeslot.'

'So why are you asking me for a preferred time, mate?'

'It's procedure sir.'

'Ok 8am then.'

'Excellent choice, sir, I'll inform Nurse Clock. And don't try to escape or she'll cut your balls off.'

From what I could see, there were no bars on the windows, and Limmy said the staff go home and leave everyone to their own devices, so a midnight runner was on the cards.

'You little depress, I understand. Me depress too,' said Karim with a ping pong ball in his hand.

'Really, you've had a lobotomy as well?'

'No, but I will hold your hand when Clock does it. Make you feel better, but I sorry, I cannot wipe arse afterwards, that Slimos job.'

'Slimo?'

'Yeah, he volunteer to clean up the vegetables on ward. He changes nappy and helps you. But maybe he wants something in return. I know nothing of those matters of course, you understand?'

'Karim, be serious, mate. I need to get out of here.'

'All good, all good, my friend. I only joke. Limmy has a plan for tonight.'

'What is it?'

'I'm not sure, but I assume he throw meat clever through the window and we escape down the road. Just my guess.'

'Nice plan, so all the hang-seng shit was a decoy mate. He was shitting everyone?'

'Yeah.'

Later that night, we arrived at the games room to find a seven-foot American Indian standing in our way, and when we asked him to move, he picked up a concrete water fountain and threw it through the window, mate. He jumped out and ran through a grassy field until we couldn't see him anymore.

'What the fuck was that all about cuz? Looked like he was working from a script or something mate.'

'Chum lover.'

'Ok, let's go then. I can see the main road from here.'

We ran through the field like Sally Field giving head on Golden Pond, with Hepburn and Fonda drooling from the sidelines.

'Put your finger out, ya dense Russian. Like this, see? You won't get anyone to stop standing like a totem pole,' I said, standing on the side of the road.

'That thumb?'

'Finger, thumb, same bloody thing.'

'Should leave you for Clock!'

'No, don't say things like that, my old Russian cuz, we're in this together. Now stick your finger out like you mean it, mate.'

'Boss car,' said Limmy.

A car pulled up with Tex and Veronica in it. We were saved, I think.

'Where the Star of David have you lot been?'

'In hospital, cuz. We did good Tex,' said Karim.

'Yeah, well, I haven't heard from Brains about your performance, so you're all gonna have to fill me in. And don't bullshit to me, because I'll know.'

'Well, the mortuary was exciting, we learned a lot about respect for the dead and how to go about everything in an ethical manner, cuz.'

'So, you fucked it up?'

'Yeah, pretty much cuz. It was Brian's fault, mate, he's a raving psycho, and the front desk lady wasn't helpful either.'

'She's my god damn niece, so don't go tongue wagging in the wrong direction.'

'She like fuck,' said Karim.

'Are you asking or telling Casanova?'

'Not sure.'

'Then shut up!'

'Where are you guys off to?' I asked.

'A swinger's party. Maybe I can get you swinging dicks in the front door.'

'So, what will we learn there, cuz? What skills I mean?'

Veronica laughed.

'Here, have some chocolates, you two. They're specially made ones. Double trouble,' said Veronica.

I wasn't sure what she meant by that, but Karim and I hoed in, and suddenly, things looked a little different. The doors began to warp, and Tex looked like a nice guy. I developed X-ray vision and could see Veronica's bra size. Then I passed out.

Chapter Eight

We woke up on a sofa with two fat grannies on top of us. One of them had her tongue so far down Karim's throat, that it got stuck on the coarse bumps of his Adam's apple mate.

'Who the fuck this?' asked Karim after pulling himself free.

'I dunno cuz, who the fuck is this chick on my lap? Looks like Jabba the Hun, mate. Mibba, bebba, ebbawonga – you no Jedi! Do you speak English fat ass?'

She slapped me and went onto the next guy.

'Jesus Christ mate, she was fatter than fuck! I can't feel my legs, mate. Tex, you dragged us here, you tyrannical Texas T-bone chestnut mare! Get over here and apologise!'

He was on the far sofa getting stuck into Veronica sideways. He looked like a god-damn supernatural American porn star or something. A real fucking performer I'm telling ya mate. It seemed like a bad idea to disturb them; in any case, I wanted to watch.

'No look, privacy,' said Karim.

'It's a swinger's party mate, and anyway, the prick

drugged us, and we've gone through God knows how many grannies' mate. That's statutory rape, cuz. We could have his wholesome Dorthy loving Kansas candy ass on ice mate.'

'Make a call police?'

'What are you fucking insane, shut up!'

Suddenly, a beautiful lady appeared from nowhere.

'Oh Vince, I'm back from the toilet, honey, and ready for some more of that rocky road loving darling. How about you and me on the floor this time?' said a very large, lady-like figure with heavy makeup, extra-large childbearing hips, and varicose veins on her neck.

'Hey?'

'You promised after I'd had a shower. Everyone heard you!'

'Promise is promise,' said Karim.

'Talk to the Yank in the doggy style position, love. He drugged us with laced chocolates, mate.'

'Fucking ye-ha girl. C'mon honey, swing those hips for your daddy young lady, and don't be skipping on the ass slapping, ya hear!' said Tex riding the living hell out of Veronica.

'Isn't Tex supposed to slap her, mate, not the other way around?'

'Sorry, I have not experienced,' replied Karim.

'Well, you could?' said the same overly large chick. 'You guys should come and work for me. Betty's my name, and I run *Freedom Town* downtown.'

'Hey, your business is free downtown, cuz?'

'No, I said it's called Freedom Town, and it's downtown.'

'Wow, a downtown free town. What do I get for free, mate?'

'Well, I can see your brain isn't why you're here. I'll say it one more time.'

'Na, don't bother love, I don't work for free, and I always stay uptown. Do you have any spare cash you can lend, mate?'

She walked away in a hurry, but I was kinda glad cuz.

'My dick hurt.'

'Well, stop playing with it cuz, you're turning off the good-looking ones on the other side of the room.'

'The ones with a bag over their head?'

'Yeah, that's them. I bet they're the hot ones, mate. They always hide behind the sofa when everyone else is shagging.'

By that time, Tex had worn out his lady. His doggy style had turned into a nail the maiden style technique that pinned the poor girl to the hard vinyl floor. She'd had enough and came and sat with us.

'Fucking yank, pushes the envelope. Just won't stop when a girl asks. And don't even think of asking Vince, I said no before I even met you.'

'What about that day in the Datsun 180B in Perth? We were virtually all over each other, mate?'

'I thought you were disabled.'

Karim laughed. He had a good memory.

'Hey Veronica, can you put in a good word for us?'

'With whom?'

'The chicks over there with the bags over their heads.'

'Are you sure?'

'Course mate, look at the bodies on them cuz? 10/10 all the way up to the neck mate.'

'So don't you want to know why they have bags over their heads?'

'All good cuz, I've got it worked out mate. It's a deception technique. They're so good-looking that they don't want to get swamped.'

'Are you sure?'

'Sure mate, get over there ya tattooed lunatic. Show me some favouritism, babe.'

'Ok, if you're sure.'

'Maybe should ask?' said Karim.

'Look mate, I know I've been through a dozen fat assed grannies, but I'm saving the best for last mate. I can feel it in my gonads.'

We sat back with our legs spread wide open for ten minutes while Veronica kept pointing over at us. The girls shook their heads every time they looked over, mate, but when Veronica said they'd be paid for it, they walked over and showed us the goods.

'Um, I think you got the wrong Vince mate.'

These girls were Star Trek fans and recently got plastic surgery to look like female Klingon warriors. Their faces were twisted and evil, mate, and their tongues came out on seven different angles in vibration mode.

'What the fuck are you cuz? Put the bags back on, now, mate, please!'

'No, Veronica said you'd pay us for a hefty shag. If you don't want to do it anymore, you still need to pay.'

'In Daktarin currency?'

They walked away shaking their heads.

'See, the grannies weren't all that bad, eh?' said Veronica, sitting back down on the sofa.

'That was weird cuz. I didn't know people got that attached to the TV.'

'That's nothing, a hooker came over earlier with venereal disease tattooed on her forehead. That's when you two were drugged out.'

Karim laughed.

'You see that granny with the love heart t-shirt?' she asked.

'Yeah mate. Hang on, why is everyone a granny around here?'

'She owns *call me* in the city.'

'Is that downtown?'

'No, it's central, you idiot. She's looking for call centre operators. Her name is Sally.'

'Karim can't speak English.'

'He'd be trained.'

'So, this is another chance to gain skills to make Mum happy?'

'Spot on kid.'

'Ok, bring her over, mate.'

'No, I'm sick of doing things for you. Go over and introduce yourselves.'

We sat there staring at this elderly lady with a love heart t-shirt. She came over after a while and asked the obvious.

'Why are you staring at me?' she asked.

'It's a swinger's party, mate.'

'Yeah, I know, we went for it at the beginning. Don't you remember?'

We sat up.

'Oh yes mate, couldn't forget it, ay. Night of my life, mate. Sally, right?'

'I didn't tell you my name.'

Karim coughed.

'Ok, Veronica said you might have a job for us. We're looking to gain skills.'

'You got a resume?'

'Yeah mate, it's the road map on my right hand, care to see?'

'Hmm. Some fight in the young fella. Well, ok, let's see if you can work better than you shag. How about you, Russian, you up for some training?'

'Hammer and sickle to the rescue.'

'What kind of work do you do, mate?'

'So, you say yes before you know what you're getting into? Smart fellas ay?'

'We are mate, we are.'

'It's a call centre. People call in and ask for advice on computer issues to dating tips. You need to be the king of bullshit, the prince of crap, the academic in a suit with patches on his elbows.'

'You got a way with words, cuzzina. We're interested. What does it pay?'

'While you're training, nothing. If you pass the trial, we'll talk business.'

We looked across the room at Tex and Veronica pissing themselves laughing.

'So, are you guys in? I need to know now.'

'Why now cuz?'

'Because we need to leave now. You can stay at my place.'

'Isn't that kinda sudden, cuz? I mean, we've only just met.'

'Na, we got to know each other pretty well when you were drugged out. I think I liked you better then actually. So, are you in or out?'

Tex motioned us to exit the room.

Ten minutes later we were roaring down the road in a 350 Chevrolet with polished centreline mags and thick shag upholstery cuz. Every time Sally changed gears, the front bonnet rose to the tune.

'It's just a car, you know. You don't have to get so excited.'

'I like it, mate. It's really fucking good ay?'

'If you masturbate back there, I'll use your hair for the clean-up.'

'No fear, Sally babe, we're here for the skills.'

She screwed up her nose and sped up. One hour later, we arrived at her place, all excited and well fed on grannies.

'Get out and open the gate. Don't mind the Rottweilers, they'll sit on command.'

'Which is?'

'I'll tell you when you get out there.'

I stood in front of the gate. The Rottweilers were going off, mate.

'Sit,' she yelled out the window.

'That's it, mate? That's the command?'

'Yeah, so? Make it simple, I say. That's the theme of my business as well. Keep everything in routine.'

When we got into the house, Sally had our beds all ready and a meal cooked.

'You can stay here tonight, then we'll go into the city. You'll get all the training you need from my colleagues.'

'Just like that, mate? Can't we sit and talk for a bit, ya know, form a relationship, cuz?'

'We've just come from a swingers' party. And by the way, why did you arrive with chocolate all over your face?'

'Long story, mate, we've got a boss with a sense of humour, ay Karim?'

'Yeah?'

'Does he speak English? He'll need to work as a call centre operator, otherwise, I've got other employment. Russian, can you say anything?'

'My arms are big and have rock balls.'

'Anything else?'

'Hammer and sickle up your ass with broken glass.'

'That's his favourite line cuz, pretty cool ay mate?'

'Yeah, not bad, but I'm not sure that would be good

advice for people who want to sort out their issues in the world. I'll have to think of something else.'

'We've got other people in the team cuz, there's Limmy and Buster mate, they can spin a yarn.'

'Yeah, I met Limmy at the swingers' party. He got upset when a chick told him he's got micro penis, then he cut off her little toe with a meat clever and put it in the microwave. Real fucking psycho mate.'

'So can he have a job with us?'

'What did I just fucking say? Get some sleep, there's work to do tomorrow.'

I could already tell she was gonna be trouble. But I was fucking excited ay cuz; an opportunity to give my El Primo Lebbo advice to the world. I was gonna be a teacher, mate. I felt important.

'What me do?' asked Karim.

'Whatever she says, mate.'

'How come I get butt fucked?'

'Well, you need to choose the right partner at parties, mate. A man and a woman look a little different, don't you know that, cuz?'

'I mean in life?'

'Oh yeah, sorry mate.'

'Look, now that I'm in the advice industry as a pre-eminent call centre dude, I can honestly say that you're just unlucky. How does that go down, mate?'

'Unlucky?'

'Yeah mate, as in someone who is lucky but not you or anyone you know.'

'Hmmm.'

'Look, you'll find your calling in life, mate. Just stick with me and everything will turn out fine. Trust me cuz.'

He looked a little dubious, but I didn't know why, cuz. I was now the master advisor of the universe, and I hadn't even been to training yet.

The next day, we were sitting on the second floor of a dingy office building in Pitt Street. There was a lady with thick glasses sitting out front taking the roll.

'Karim? Are you here?'

'Yeah.'

'What's your last name, love?'

'No, not love.'

'No, I mean what's your last name?'

'Ivanov.'

'Great name, love. Do you know any tennis players?'

He didn't answer.

'And how about you love?' she asked me.

'Yeah, I'm fine.'

'No, what's your name, love?'

'Lombardi, Vince Lombardi.'

She went through the whole class doing the 'love' thing until Sally rocked up.

'Well, I think I know most of you. I'm Sally, and I'm the director. This company is all about giving advice to those in need. There are no formal requirements as such, just your experience in life. Most of our clients just need someone to talk to. The first floor is all admin, the second is the call centre, and the third is out of bounds to anyone not invited. Please don't try and use the elevator to get up there as you'll need a code. It's all very hush hush and mind your own fucking business type thing, so don't even ask or I'll bop you.'

'What's the third floor used for, mate?'

'Excuse me??'

'Ah, I'm just fucking with ya cuz, just like at the swingers party last night ay mate?'

She ignored me.

'During the day, you'll be divided up between admin, the call centre, and hush-hush stuff. If any of you are willing to put up your hand for the third floor without asking what's up there or what you'll be doing, then please speak up now.'

'So, what's up there?' asked a foreign exchange student.

'None of your business.'

'What do you do up there?' asked a single mother with Ugg boots on nursing a crying baby.

'Who wants to know?'

Silence.

'Well, if there aren't any more questions, I'll take you, you, and you to the third floor. Now get your asses moving.'

'Me again?' asked Karim.

'Tough luck mate. It's probably some cushy job peeling bananas, or painting pot plants, or something. You'll be right, mate,' I said, slapping him on the back.

Karim took the elevator with two other thick-set Slovakian types.

'Now, this job involves people calling in for advice on matters of concern. They will usually be relationship-based or similar. Don't be afraid to give your opinion on what's required. This is mainly a talk line, for those who are lonely and want someone to hold their hand, so that's why you don't need any qualifications. Everyone understand?'

'Someone said yes in Chinese.'

'So, can all ten of you please go into the next room and wait at your desk. The calls should be coming in soon, and don't worry, this lovely lady will be here to ask for advice.'

'Yes, love, thank you, love doll. I'll do all I can to help you guys whilst you're here. Let's be as professional as possible, and no eating my fucking mars bars from the fridge, ok?'

Someone farted.

'I've got a question, cuz. What happens on the third floor?'

'In the room, Lebbo boy. Watch him, he's trouble,' said Sally to the love babe.

I sat there for half an hour before the phones began to ring. The lady next to me got caught up in a love triangle conversation and asked me why it was called a love triangle.

'It's about the dynamics, mate, ya know, three angles all part of one mathematical formula, mate. It's the angles that count, ya know, and how they bounce off each other.'

'Ok, you take the call,' she said.

'Na mate, go and ask the love child in the room over there. And take a Mars bar from the fridge before ya get there.'

Ring, ring!

'What's that?' I asked.

'The phone love, pick it up.'

'But what do I say, mate? What if I get into something dirty, or advise some poor kid to join the navy, or convince a no-hoper to run for parliament or something?'

'Just be yourself love, and don't tell people to touch my fucking mars bars!'

I picked up the phone and gave a false name.

'Hey cuz lad, babe or whatever the fuck ya name is. How are we today?'

'I must fix my computer,' said a voice on the other line.

'Ok, fix it then.'

He sounded Indian.

'I mean, there is something wrong with your computer. Can you please get in front of your computer?'

'Na mate, look, you've got it all wrong. I'm in a call centre.'

'So am I. Can you please turn on your computer?'

'Ok mate, there you go.'

'Ok, can you hit the Windows button and type in the following command?'

'Ok mate.'

'69cumonme.exe'

'Done.'

'Ok, now look at the history and tell me what you see.'

'There are three transactions to pay for women's nickers.'

'Yes, sir, I see that too, can you see the credit card number that was used?'

'Yes, it's all here, except the security code on the back of the card, mate, do you want it?'

'Yes please.'

'It says I need to add a subsidiary card to view the security code of the first one, mate.'

'Subsidiary sir?'

'Yeah, another card mate. I've left mine at home. Can I have yours cuz?'

'I'm not sure I'm allowed to, sir.'

'It's just for a minute. Once I enter your details, it will show me the security code of the first one, mate, promise cuz!'

The guy gave me his credit details, and I bought $6000 worth of Mars bars from Woolworths online.

'Excuse me, sir, are you still there? Can I have the security code, please?'

'Check ya balance mate!!'

I hung up. It was good to get back at the bastards that con other bastards to buy shit stuff online. I felt good about myself. Twenty minutes later, the love babe came over to my desk.

'Vince, there are sixty-seven boxes of Mars bars on the first floor addressed to 'love babe,' is that me?'

'How'd ya guess? It's my present to you, mate.'

'Love ya wog boy!'

I was in a mate. My line manager loved my guts cuz. She threw a couple of bite-sized bars my way from time to time, but for the most part, she stuffed her face with the caramel delights every chance she got, mate. That kept her away from me and her mouth shut.

'If she is always there in the office eating chocolate, she might get sack,' said an international student next to me.

'Why?'

'She's eating Mars bars all day, no longer an advice person, you see.'

'Yeah, we can deal with it, cuz.'

All the while, I could hear this squeaking sound on the third floor, which sounded like mice getting strangled, mate. Really fucking weird. I just hoped Karim and his Slovak friends were ok.

The next call came in around 1 pm, and I picked him for a rich fella, cuz. He talked about needing hospital care and being stressed out at work all the time.

'All these meetings are getting me worked up. I own so many companies now that I can't keep track of anything. Even the news networks are owned by me, and some of the newspapers. I need to find some free medical cover to take care of my body. Any suggestions?'

'Excuse me, cuz, sorry, what's your name?'

'Laurie Slacker. I own channel 10 and just about everything else I can see, which is probably why it belongs to me. Now this is an advice hotline, so what's your advice.'

'Hang on.'

I went over to Love Babe's office, but she was stuffing herself with Mars bars. She'd gone through five boxes in an hour. Now that's dedication, cuz.

'Um, I'm sorry, sir, but I will need to meet with you in person. Can I come to your office?' I asked.

'Yes, that's ok, come to the fourth floor at 54 Park Street. And don't con onto my secretary, I'm banging her three times a day so she's not into you, forget it!'

'That's fine, sir cuz, because I'm a regular at the fat babe Klingon swinger's party. I'm all satisfied, mate.'

'Well, that's one I haven't been to. I'll talk to you when you get here.'

I walked down Pitt Street until another street that connected with mine started with P, and low and behold, mate, it was Park Street. I was fucking proud of myself. I got the elevator to the third floor without asking for help, and a nice lady with an even nicer dress asked me if I was a virgin, or it might have been if I flew Virgin Airways. I was too fucking nervous to pay much attention.

'This is the third floor, sir, you'll need a passcode access to visit any higher.'

'So, you're the secretary that my client is banging three times a day?'

'Excuse me sir?'

'Forget it, what's the passcode?'

'Sorry, I can't tell you that, sir.'

'Ah, it's ok, I'll work it out.'

I got back into the elevator, and it prompted me to enter a six-digit password. I put in six zeros, and it let me go up. For all the money this guy had, he couldn't think of anything more complicated? Or perhaps it was my genius IQ and sleek aptitude, mate.

'Excuse me, love, are you the love babe that smiles when her breasts get squeezed?'

'Yes, sir, that's me. Please come closer so I can identify you.'

She slapped me so hard that my head did a 180-degree turn.

'Slacker slave babe. I was only going off what your

boss was saying, mate. Apologise right now or I'll tell everyone you've got Chinese sex dolls hidden under your bed.'

'Oh no, please, the parcel was a mistake, sir. I never meant to open it.'

'Ah, that's alright, babe. But tell me, why do you need a sex doll if you're being banged three times a day?'

She slapped me again.

'Call centre boy, front and centre,' said Mr. Slacker from his office.

I entered a large office with trophy heads all over the walls and thick shag carpet on the floor. I counted three air conditioners, six chairs made of ivory, three broken guitars, and a large-scale model of an oil rig on his desk. The guy was a fucking nutcase mate.

'Sit down boy.'

'The name is Vince Mr. Slacker, how are you?'

'Why?'

'Because you called me for advice.'

'Oh yes, I remember now. How are you?'

'Ah yeah, I'm good mate.'

'So, what should I do about this health insurance thing? I've got money to burn, but I don't want to burn it. You see my problem?'

'Yeah, you're a rich tight-ass that's chocked full of shit mate.'

'That's what my wife says, any further advice?'

'Na.'

'You know anyone with a spare kidney?' he asked.

'Mum said I might have a spare down my pants, but I haven't seen her for a while.'

'Ok, rip it out and leave it on the desk. C'mon, I'm busy.'

The guy was serious, and I was seriously thinking about how to make it happen, mate.

'What about the shag meister secretary outside?'

'I've worked her too hard, the doc said no.'

'Well, they're you go cuz, you soil your royal oats for too long and the babes get put out to pasture mate. I hope you've learnt your lesson, cuz?'

'Fuck off.'

By the time I got back to the elevator, the security guy had changed the password, so I put in five zeros and a one, and it let me down. I walked past the guy on the first floor with my middle finger waving high and proud. He couldn't do anything as he had one hand stuck in his turban and the other up his ass. I felt we could've been friends.

I made myself a promise that I wouldn't leave the office again, but when I returned, the Mars bar love child wanted to see me.

'Sit down,' she said with chocolate all over her mouth.

'I've got a better …'

'Better?'

'Better … better get a bucket, I'm gonna throw up.'

'Um, I don't think I know where one is, mate. You'd better chuck on the floor, then you can clean it up afterwards.'

She chucked for three minutes then wiped her mouth.

'You bastard, you did this to me!'

'Well, if you weren't such a gluttonous pig, then my little Mars bar escapade would've failed, mate, don't you think?'

'You're still a bastard.'

'No, I have a mum, and she lives on the north shore. Any further comments?'

'Yes, a guy called Tommy phoned you. He's got no fashion sense and wants to meet you on the corner of Park and Pitt.'

'I've just fucking come from there. Anyway, this is a call centre mate, you know, where calls come in?'

'He's paying for it, so he gets it.'

'You mean like a geriatric who wants to shag a blonde 18 year old model?'

'Exactly, now get to it.'

'Right, where is she?'

'It's a he! Now stop buying me mars bars and piss off.'

I left hearing those mouse-like sounds from the top floor again.

I arrived at the corner of Park and Pitt and saw a zombie-like figure standing in the middle of the road. He's been smoking crack for sure cuz.

'Ay, Tommy, are you out of it?'

'Aw yeah man, yeah sure.'

He approached me and stuck his tongue in my ear.

'What? Get out of it, mate.'

'Yeah, I'm out for it mate, let's rock!' said Tommy.

'I said, are you out of it? Can't you understand, cuz? The agency called and said you needed some fashion advice, but it looks like you need more than that, ay cuz'

'Hey, don't be ragging on the outskirts of society, my man. I'm a product of my environment, mate. Can't you see?'

'You sound educated.'

'I am my man, that's why I'm so successful, see!'

'I don't think I can help you, cuz.'

'You're a call centre dude, my man, you can do anything!'

I wasn't aware of my newly found reputation, mate, but I felt a sense of obligation to live up to his expectations.

'Ok so fashion sense ay? Are you sure?'

'Sure, my man, very sure. If you come with me down Pitt Street, we can go into a clothes shop and try some stuff on. If they see you, they might let me in as well.'

'Because I'm suave, mate?'

'No, because they'll be scared of you, my man.'

I began to get self-conscious.

'You mean it's my accent, the way I walk, my attitude?'

'Na, just joshing with ya, my man. Strength in numbers, young Lebbo. We can do it.'

I trusted the guy like a snake teased with a stick. But it was my job to teach him some fashion sense, and in no time, we found a shop called *Tinkle Boy Town* in the heart of the CBD.

'Oh, young men with something to hide, ay? Looks

like fun on a stick, ay Reggy?' said a small thin guy as we entered.

'Oh yes, oh yes, oh my god, such deliverance and yet so much goodness to be found. Oh my god, what do we have here?' said his friend from behind the counter, flapping his hands about.

'We're here to get some fashion sense, young cuzzinas. Young Tommy here wants to learn about it mate.'

'Paying by cash? Diners, Mastercard, Visa?'

'Well, can that be negotiated, cuz?'

The shop attendants looked at each other.

'Oh my god, well of course it can, you little love creatures. Set back the dial, Reggy, cause we're coming through, love children! The name's Mario, my new bonk lads. Let me have a look at you.'

He twirled us around like a bullied ballerina coach.

'Yeah, oh my god, Reggy lad, look at this Laddy. What's your name Sonny?'

'Vince, mate, but Tommy's the one who needs it, not me.'

'Oh, what do you think, Reggy? Should we accommodate or set him free outside?'

'Looks nice,' replied Reggy.

'Ok, the man behind the till has spoken with the nicest of manners. I must say, oh my god, I can't forget the first time I saw this man, oh my god, standing by the till in another store, so handsome, so well dressed.'

'Agree with that, Mario man. Love ya like a sister!' replied Reggy, filing his fingernails.

'Ok, cuz boys, after all that, what can we try on mate?'

'Oh well, let's see, oh my god, there's so much to do and so little time. Reggy, lock the door, my cash management sweetie. Let's work on Tommy the homeless lad and make him a star.'

'Well, there's my promise made good, young Tommy, anything else?' I asked,

'Na, my man, but I need you to stick around for a while. I'm not feeling too well and the boys in this shop are giving me funny looks.'

'They're harmless, Tommy. Anyway, I need to get

back to the call centre. Let me know how you go, cuz.'

Tommy fainted and fell on the floor.

'We'll take care of him, my cuz Laddy, oh my god, come back soon!'

I wondered if I was doing the right thing by leaving him there alone, mate, but it wasn't my job to see the end outcome. I was there to give advice, mate, and I needed to get back to the office.

When I got back, the love child Mars bar babe, wanted to see me again.

She was sitting there with three buckets of spew next to her.

'How you feeling, cuz babe?'

'Better.'

'Better get a bucket?'

'No, I feel better. Don't be funny. Anyway, how did it go with Tommy?'

'Good mate, excellent, couldn't have gone any better.'

'Which means?'

'I left him with two twinkle boys in the city.'

'The Twinkle boys, from Twinkle Town!'

'Yes, so fucking what cuz, is there a problem?'

'Nope, no problem at all. Just wanted to know, that's all. Have you had a lunch break?'

'Actually, I wanted to talk with Karim. Is he around?'

'He's up on the third floor.'

'Can I go up?'

'You need a passcode.'

'Let me guess, five zeros?'

'Oh, crazy, how did you know that? That's incredible!'

'Yes, isn't it, mate. Well, I'm going up, and what's that squeaky sound I keep hearing?'

'Mice.'

'Are you sure. There it is again, mate. Sounds like bedsprings snapping.'

'You mean people are going for it?'

'Maybe, do you have anything to tell me before I get up there?'

'Yeah, maybe there are people going for it?'

'Anything else, mate?'

'I like Mars bars.'

'And…'

'And you can go up there if you want.'

When I opened the elevator door, I was shocked, mate. I couldn't believe that a grown adult couldn't go out and buy a mousetrap.

'How many did you catch, Karim?'

'Twenty, but Slovakians are up by ten. Shit me.'

'You'd better get your act together, mate. If Limmy were here, he'd have caught em all in the first ten minutes.'

'And eat.'

'Yeah, most likely mate. Anyway, this place is weird cuz. Let's get our paychecks and get out of here.'

I went back to see the Mars bar cuz, but she'd had a

heart attack and been taken to hospital. There was a box of Mars bars on her desk with my name on it, so I considered it payment in full and walked out, mate.

'We need to get back into the bubble bath industry,' I said, chomping on a Mars bar.

'Yeah, back to Tex and ask?'

'Na, I reckon I'll go back and ask Tommy. I wanna see what he's wearing anyway.'

'When I arrived back at *Twinkle Town*, the boys were dumping Tommy out the back, naked from head to toe.'

'Oh my god, Vince cuz, oh laddy, he wouldn't cooperate at all,' said Reggy.

'How did he get naked, mate?'

'He stripped off the clothes we gave him and fainted again. I offered him coffee, biscuits, and apple cider. Reggy played the flute and sang Elmore James tunes, then I whistled Advance Australia fair, but no-go jo blow, and here he is. Why, don't you believe me?'

'I do,' said Karim.

'Oh, you're a lovely Russian, aren't you, honey,

sweet nectar lover. Would you like to try some clothes on, sweetie?'

We looked at Tommy, passed out on the ground.

'Yeah, ok,' said Karim.

'Ah na mate, sorry, we've gotta be somewhere cuz.'

'Ok, you're loss, babes, seeya!'

They went back inside and slammed the door. Tommy was semiconscious at that stage and asked for help to get dressed.

'Oh, careful, my man, it's tender there. I think the lads tried me on.'

'You mean the whole heave ho in the change room?'

'No, my man, I mean the jeans were too tight. Skinny jeans don't agree with me.'

'So where do you want to go, cuz?'

'Just leave me here, my man, the twinkle boys will come out later and buy me some food. They owe me. Where are you boys off to?'

'We wanna get back into the bubble bath industry

cuz.'

'Selling dope my man?'

'How did you know, mate?'

'I know the lingo, my man. Here, go and see my mate *Man*. He's got a plantation in Manly. He'll show you the ropes, my man. Just say Tommy sent you. Here's his business card. He's into the dope big time, my man.'

'What if he knows two people called Tommy cuz?'

'Then you explain what I look like, my man.'

'Ow yeah, I guess, mate, good thinking. Are you sure his name is Man?'

'He's the man, my man!'

We left Tommy flat on his stomach at the back of Twinkle Town and caught a taxi to Manly. The driver wanted payment before we left, but I said we knew Reggy and Mario. He looked me over and gave a wink.

Chapter Nine

We were getting back into the bubble bath scene and loving it. This was easy pie money, mate; all we had to do was deliver and collect. It's a decent way to make a living. All I needed to do was keep it a secret from me mum and lie when she asked me what my profession was. I'd probably say something like 'Aw yeah, cuz mum mate, the bubble is a booming industry, ay? Forget the shit at the supermarket that costs three dollars a bottle, we can sell it in powder form for three million percent more. I'm tipping she's gonna believe me ay mate, just depends on my bullshit lingo level, and suave attitude.

When we arrived at *Man's* house, we saw an ocean of scrub on both sides, mate. The breeze whistled through the dope trees and made us feel at home. This was our new profession, mate, we could feel it.

'Hey, Essay, you got lost or something, Holmes?' said a guy from his bedroom window.

'Hey, mate, is that you, Mr. Man? Sorry man, if it's not. Tommy sent us from the city,' I said.

'You making fun of my name, man?'

'If it's you, man, then, no way.'

'Get the fuck off my property Essay.'

'Look, sorry man, I mean Mr. Man, can we start again?'

'I dunno, can we?'

'Yes, ok,' said Karim.

'Hey, essay, are you Russian?'

'Yes.'

'Hey man, I've got some really fucking good Russian shit in here if you wanna taste of home Holmes.'

'You keep homeless shit in your bedroom mate?'

'I ain't fucking talking to you Holmes, I'm talking to the KGB dorkarama next to you.'

'Me no dork.'

'Well then, get in here, essay, and bring your rocky road friend with you.'

The inside of the house looked like the outside. There were plants everywhere, and the smell was toxic, mate. It was like walking through a forest of incense.

'Hey, essay, watch the Mexican varieties man, they're like gold around these parts. And don't step on the Japanese Bonsai plants either, man.'

'Look good.'

'No shit Russian man. You wanna try some of this?'

'Sure.'

We sat at the kitchen table and *Man* took out some pills from his tie-dye bag.

'Hey, cuz, that's not weed, ay?'

'Ah yeah man, the Russian stuff is lethal man, so you gotta take some pills to soften the blow essay.'

I picked up a bag pills from the table.

'Like these cuz?'

'Are yeah, I think so, man, hang on, let me read up on it for a minute.'

He foraged through the kitchen cupboards and came back with a book.

'Ah, yeah, white, blue, red, yeah man, that's it, the

white one.'

'Are you sure, mate?'

'Yeah, man, here's one for you, Russian. Toke it up Holmes!'

'Water mate?' I asked.

'Sorry, essay, not connected.'

It went down dry mate. We had to use our saliva to get it all the way down.

'Hey man, wait a minute, don't take those. I almost gave you the wrong stuff essay.'

'Hey, what are you talking about, cuz? You looked in the book, right? What's the book say, give it to me, cuz.'

The title read: How to Cook for Dopers.

'This is a fucking cookbook cuz. Look!'

'Hey man, I'm really sorry, dudes, I'll make it up to you.'

'So, what pill?' asked Karim.

'I'm not so sure, man, I'll need to consult my book.'

He looked in the cookbook.

'I think it's just paracetamol, man, I'm sure of it, ay essay.'

'Are you sure cuz?'

'Ah, not really, but if you start the whole head spin spew routine, then I'll help you.'

We sat there smoking Russian pot for an hour, only to be told later it was Man's recycled tea leaves. This guy was pissing me off mate.

'So, you guys know Tommy hey?' said Man after taking a piss in the laundry basket.

'Kind of mate. He asked me for advice on fashion.'

'Why didn't he call me, man?'

'Not sure, why didn't he?'

The man scratched his beard for five minutes without answering.

'Well, essay, it's like this…'

We waited for another five minutes.

'Hey, cuz, are you ok, man?'

He was spaced out, mate, like a doper that smoked recycled tea leaves.

'So, why did Tommy send you here man?' asked Mr. Man.

'He said you could show us the ropes, mate, top to bottom and inside out. Do you have time, mate?'

'Yeah, sure, essay, wait here.'

He went back into his bedroom and came back with a rope.

'Ok man, this is a rope and here is the bottom. I'm not sure where the top is, man, but I know it's not anywhere near the bottom. I've looked several times before.'

'Na mate, the doper industry. How to grow and sell cuz.'

'Oh, na man, you've been given a doper steer essay. I just live here on my own. I don't know where the pot comes from.'

'So how did you get thousands of dope plants outside your house mate?'

'Well, that's a good question, man. I think the seeds just fell out of the sky one day after I noticed a truck overturned up on the highway. The seeds must have blown down on this property, man. It all started one year ago. I haven't left the house since then essay.'

'That's it, mate. We need to cause a truck accident and hope the fucking thing is full of dope seeds that blow our way? Are you insane?'

'Most likely man, it's hard to tell when you're stoned all the time. It's kinda like an avoidance technique in life, man. Whenever someone asks you a question, you can either refer to a cookbook or keep smoking, man, it's perfect.'

'So, what can you teach us? We want to learn the ropes.'

'I just showed you essay.'

'No, skills mate, c'mon cuz?'

'Alright, essay, I'm not supposed to tell you, but I've got a plan you can help me with. I was stoned for five days straight last week, and I got an idea, man.'

'Great cuz. Does it involve a cookbook and a rope?'

'Na man, get real essay. It's about transportation to another place, in another time, man.'

'Hey?'

'Taking the plants and selling them to people, man.'

'Wow, cuz, what a drug-dealing brainstorm, mate. You're a fucking genius.'

'Hey thanks essay.'

'So, when do we start, mate?'

'Not today, I need to go to dopers anonymous. You wanna come?'

'I've never heard of that mate?'

'Yeah, apparently, I got busted with a tin of weed in a 7/11 store a month ago. I can't remember anything, man. The court ordered me to attend therapy, man. I don't remember that either.'

'So, how did you remember today?'

'I wrote it down somewhere, man. Oh, here essay, it's in the cookbook under Man's things to cook and do. Here it is, see.'

'Oh, that's really good mate. Karim, can we leave now, please?'

'Na man, it's ok, we're just getting to know each other. Come on down to dopers anonymous and help me out, ay. Then I'll tell you my plan, man.'

'So where is this place, mate?'

'No fucking idea man.'

'What time does it start?'

'Can't tell ya that essay.'

'Whose gonna be there, cuz?

'Aw yeah, yeah man, there's gonna be other people.'

'No shit cuz.'

The phone rang. He parted two Mexican dope plants and picked up the receiver.

'Hey man.'

'Ah yes, hello, can I speak to Mr. Man, please?'

'Hey man.'

'No, I'm sorry, I need to speak to Mr. Man, please.'

'Yeah man.'

'Sorry I can I speak to him?'

'Sure, man, go ahead, man.'

'Oh, I'm sorry, sir, there seems to be some kind of miscommunication. Are you Mr. Man, born on the 4 July?'

'Yeah man.'

'Oh, I'm sorry, Mr. Man, I'm glad we got that sorted. Do you remember the incident that unfolded on 17 April at the local 7/11 store?'

'Vaguely.'

'Well, you're due to attend dopers anonymous today, did you know that?'

'Oh yeah, essay. I was just talking about that with my new friends. Can you speak to them about it?'

'Why, sir, I have you on the line, and this is very confidential.'

The man pressed the speaker phone button.

'Ok man, go for it.'

'Um, I'm sorry, Mr. Man, are we now on a speaker phone?'

'Na.'

'Alright then, please be at the *barn yard* on Trump Street at 3pm today. We look forward to seeing you there, Mr. Man.'

'Oh, can I bring some support, man? I'm feeling a bit

nervous ay essay?'

'That's fine, Mr. Man, we'll see you then.'

'Aw mate, lucky they called ay man? 3 pm at the barn dance, man, got it?'

We rocked up at the *bard yard* therapy center four hours later. It was nothing like we imagined, mate, with cows and chickens all around, and bales of hay lined up on the inside walls. A real fucking surprise, I'm telling ya.

'It's now 3 pm, subjects, please take a chair and form a semi-circle,' said a stiff in a suit. 'Those supporting the subjects may join in if they please. Chop-chop, there's lots to talk about.'

This guy was smart, mate, I could tell by the blazer he was wearing – a checked tweed with patched elbows. He may have had a tobacco pipe in his front pocket, but it could've been something else, mate.

'Now this is the first *Dopers Anonymous* for this group. I realize that some of you may be nervous, so I don't want to overload you. Can we please go around the circle and say one word about how you came to be here today? How about you, Mr. Man, is it?'

'What?'

'No, I mean, is that your name?'

'Yeah man.'

The stiff paused for a second.

'Ok then, Mr. Man, please think of one word that describes why you're here.'

'Um, wow man, that's kinda heavy essay. Well, maybe 'car'.

'Car? I'm sorry, I don't understand, why car?'

'That's how I came to be here, man. Isn't that what you meant?'

'No, I mean, why are you here?'

'Well, the piggy mother fucker stole my tin man. I had the dope all pushed to one side so the papers could fit in. I was really pissed man, especially after he called me a loser in front of the checkout operator. I was making progress with the girl man, and he came along and fucked it all up.'

'So, Mr. Man, can we summarize that all into one meaningful word?'

'Na, I don't think so, essay.'

'So, the word is essay? You believe there is more to come? A fitting word,' said the stiff.

'Ah yeah man. Essay, yeah. Did you read that in my cookbook?'

The guy looked shaken.

'Now, seeing as Mr. Man has taken up all the allocated time for that part, we'll skip straight to the summaries. Please stand up at the podium and talk about your life.'

'You mean me man?'

'No, Mr. Man, I think you've taken up enough time already. How about you, I'm sorry, what's your name?'

'Lombardi mate, Vince Lombardi.'

'Please take your place at the podium.'

I was kinda nervous mate, and I wasn't sure what to say, but I'd think of something.

'Um, hello.'

'Hello Vince,' they said collectively.

'Well, my experience in the doper scene is limited.

I've stolen a 1970s TV from a helpless granny, shoved Vodka up a dead man's ass, sold piss to a boxing crowd telling them it was water, and shagged old ladies on chocolate laced magic mushrooms. Any comments?'

'Thank you, Vince,' they answered collectively.

'Excuse me, stiff cuz, are they going to say that every time someone speaks?'

'It's validation, Mr. Lombardi. Everyone needs to feel they are listened to for salvation to seep into their very core.'

'You mean hardcore mate?'

'Sit down Mr. Lombardi.'

'So, who's next? Mr. Man, how about you?'

'That's me man.'

'No, Mr. Man, it's your time to speak.'

'I did, man,' he said, chomping on a discounted chocolate bar. 'How about the Russian dude, he looks interesting.'

'Na.'

'Oh, come on .. Mr.?'

'Ivanov.'

'He can't speak English properly cuz.'

'Oh no, Mr. Lombardi, this simply won't do. I won't have blasphemy in my group sessions.'

'How is it blasphemy, mate? You're not God, and neither is Russia. You're not making sense, stiff cuz.'

'What I meant to say, little man, was that we are all equal in my eyes.'

'Hey, that's a God saying. You're a stinking preacher boy, aren't ya?'

He ripped off his jacket and patched elbows to reveal a white necked collar. It's what we all expected.

'Run everyone, flee cuz dudes, he's trying to connect us to God. If you get up there, he won't let you back down, take my word for it, mate.'

Man was the first one out the door as the stiff preacher dude prayed for our sins on his knees.

'Hey, thanks, essay, that was kinda cool, man. You're on the level with the lip stuff, man. You got the lingo shit talk.'

'Well, I do my best, man, cuz. I am the lyrical gangster, the plain-clothed officer, the universal soldier, and …'

'Full of shit,' said Karim.

I was impressed mate. The Russian fuck had finished one of my sentences. He was moving up in the world.

'Hey thanks essays. You're cool dudes, ay?' said Man.

'So now you'll teach us, mate?'

'About?'

'The idea you had, mate. Here's your cookbook. Did you write it in there somewhere?'

He studied the pages for a while, flipping each one as if he were only looking at the pictures, mate.

'Aw yeah man. It's my master plan. Na, hang on, that's how to make Tabouleh salad.'

'Let me see that. Hmmm…no ginger in this one. I'll have to ask Mum when I see her.'

'Ah, na, hang on, here it is. Yeah, man, it's my top-secret plan essay.'

'Awesome mate, what is it?'

'I can't tell ya, it's a secret.'

'No, you said you would.'

'Tell you my top-secret plan about the grand scheme of things?'

'No, about dope dealing mate.'

'Oh, that top secret plan. Yeah, ok, let's get back to the house and I'll spell it out, mate.'

'No, let's do it here, mate. If we wait until then, you'll forget.'

'True man, true.'

Man bonged on for the best part of an hour when we got home. He had all his stash divided by nationality. Karim said it was racist, but I didn't think so. After a while, Man passed out in his bedroom, but Karim threw a cup of water on his balls and said the roof was leaking. Man bought the whole deal and came out to the kitchen table with his cookbook under his arm.

'Ok man dudes, here we go.'

I shivered with anticipation.

'Chicken carbonara man!'

'No, you idiot, the drug deal plan.'

'Ah yes.'

He flicked through a few more pages.

'Here we are. Now you see that forest plantation of dope trees on either side of the house?'

'Ay, yeah mate.'

'Well, it might get to a stage where someone might notice man. Any suggestions?'

'That's it,' asked Karim.

'Well, Russian laddy, there's only so many spare pages in a cookbook, isn't there, man!'

'Ok, I have an idea cuz. You see those empty houses on stilts next to this house?' I asked.

'Na man.'

'Then look out the fucking window mate.'

'Oh yeah, essay, where did they come from?'

'Well, we fill the houses chock-a-block with dope and drive them to a paying customer. We'll hire escorts so the cops will never expect a thing, mate. They'll think we're just transporting empty houses.'

'Who's the customer man?'

'Anyone who wants to buy it, mate. We'll put up signs on the houses saying *for sale* or something.'

'Then people will notice man.'

'So, don't use the signs, whatever mate.'

Man scratched his chin for a while until I told him to stop.

'The idea has potential, man, real potential. Let me give my mate Tommy a call down on Pitt Street. Do you know him essay?'

'Na mate, never heard of him cuz.'

'Well, he's a cool dude. Not sure if he's up and able these days, though. Rumour has it he sells himself to male clothes shop assistants for free advice, man. Know anything about that?'

'Not a thing cuz.'

'How about you, Russian man?'

'Dunno.'

'Ok, tomorrow morning we'll start work. I've got

some machetes in the back room. We'll hoe into the plantation and stuff the houses, choko man. Russian, you call the escorts and make a booking. We're gonna make a fortune, ay essay?'

'Assuming we can cut down a whole plantation of weed with machetes in one day, and assuming Karim makes the call, and whether hookers come instead of escorts for the wide load cuz?'

'Don't be pessimistic, my olive skin tyrant. All will come together in a concoction of bliss flavored syrup and willpower, man. I've read it in my book.'

'The recipe book mate?'

'Um, let me check. Yes, it has recipes in it, what's your point?'

I was seriously thinking of using his cookbook to wipe my ass mate.

'Ok, man, why don't I just yell our plan out the window cuz, because then in the morning the whole plantation will be in the spare houses, and our escorts will be waiting, mate. We'll only need to have breakfast, which you can use your recipe book for,' I said in a sarcastic tome.

'Man, you are the organizer of the history of all organizational stuff. You've written the book, man, many times over. I'll need to get some recipes off you, ay? But what if someone hears you and calls the cops, essay?'

'Karim, deal with this fella, will ya?'

'I fix, let me go out onto the road. I have an ancient technique.'

'Ok, do it. I'm sleeping right on this sofa cuz.'

The next morning, Karim was standing over me with escorts, ready to get going.

'Karim mate, you're a fucking genius.'

'Houses are full, escorts ready to go, so let go.'

'Let go of what?'

'I mean, let's go.'

Man walked out of his bedroom with a teddy under his arm.

'Russian honey dew love child. You did it man. Look at all those houses full of weed essay. How did you do it man?' asked Man wearing his *fueled by bananas* pajamas.

'I walk over hill and put message in bottle.'

'And threw it out to sea, man?'

'And throw into moving car. The window breaks, and I run away. Down the road, the lady catches up and say, *you missed the ocean*. I say, 'I throw dream to the wind, and hit.'

'Are you sure cuz? That sounds a little far-fetched, mate.'

'Freaky man, really freaky essay. But I have heard of such ways the universe can sway and alter reality, man. It's in my cookbook.'

'Yes, but how does it explain a whole plantation of weed getting into the houses?'

'Oh, man, I think it may have already been there. My landlord said I could get free rent if I kept it safe. Look, the plantation is still there, man.'

I took a closer look, and they were Chinese tea trees.

'So, your landlord said we can sell it cuz?'

'I didn't hear him say that, man, but I could check. I've got his phone number somewhere. I think I wrote it down in my cookbook, man.'

'Fuck it mate. So, where are we taking these three houses full of weed?'

'Somewhere casual man. A quiet place man.'

'So, no one will see us and we'll have to bring it back, mate?'

'Need to rethink,' said Karim.

'Pitt Street man. Maybe we'll see Tommy and he can point us in the right direction, essay.'

'You mean to a clothes shop for fashion advice, mate?'

'He's our only contact. We need someone to buy the weed, man. Unless you want to put up your signs?'

'Fuck it cuz, let's just go.'

We travelled at snail's pace down the road with three houses and a wide load escort. It took four hours to reach Pitt Street, and when we got there, the businesses were preparing to shut down for the day, mate.

'We're too late essay.'

'Late for what cuz?'

'Too late for something, whatever, man. I need a hit man. Going out back.'

He looked disappointed mate, really fucking cut. But if he had more common sense, he'd be a lot fucking happier. That was my deduction anyway, mate.

Mr. Man returned ten minutes later, stoned to the max, mate.

'What smell?' asked Karim.

'Ah yeah, sorry I didn't offer you any essays, I'm a bit short these days. Dry times man.'

I looked at the three houses full of weed.

'So, what is that smell, cuz?'

'Told you man.'

'Na mate, there's smoke coming from the back house cuz.'

'So, there is man. Looks good ay?'

It didn't take long for all three houses to go up in flames, mate. Smoke poured into Pitt Street, sending everyone into a state of ecstasy. People started asking for Twisties and Corn chips, and the pub got mobbed by twenty people with a hard-on asking for *AC/DC* songs. This was some potent stuff, but no buyer would fork out cash for burning weed.

'Hey man, look at em roll out of the Commonwealth Bank man, they're really fucking out of it ay. Doing Pilates stretches and singing Beatles songs. I wanna piece of that?' said Man with a hanky over his mouth.

'You mean the money cuz?'

'Na, the dancing man. The beautiful singing.'

'I better idea,' said Karim.

He stole a small van from a wasted businessman and ram raided it into the bank.

'Help, c'mon let us go,' said Karim.

'He's a smart man, he's your friend essay?'

'It's payday, my hippy friend, let's go, mate!'

When we got back to Man's house, I counted 350 million dollars in cash.

'Who counted this man?'

'Me mate, and I'm not counting it again.'

'Na man, but how did you count it?'

'I made a pile of 100,000, then counted 350 piles the same shape mate.'

'But there's only one pile, man.'

'So?'

'So, man, it means you counted the same pile 350 times. It's only a million essay.'

'Makes sense,' said Karim.

I was embarrassed, but I didn't care cuz. We were a million dollars richer, and I was the mastermind, or perhaps it was Karim, or Man. But fuck it, I was spending my share of the money on something cool mate, perhaps for my Mum who most likely needed something to do with Mum stuff, or my 275 cousins who I couldn't remember anything about mate, or my dad who was still locked up in Lebanon for posting a picture of the local Imam in a dress. I had lots of ideas, mate, rolling around in my head, like a cane toad doing backflips in the wet season heat. I was potent, on fire, and a million dollars richer cuz.

'So, we divide the money cuz?'

'Na man, we can turn a million dollars into 350 million man.'

'You mean by counting it the wrong way, mate?'

'Yeah, I mean, na man. Tommy got wind of the robbery, and he sent me a text. He's got a deal for us essay.'

'Um, best keep him out of the equation, mate. Can't we just divide the money and split, cuz?'

'Na Holmes, it's the universe calling essay, the world has collapsed and reassembled in a billion shards of light, man, all for us in slow motion, with twinkle stars and cherry bells.'

'Let's go Karim.'

'Na, Tommy will be here soon. He's got a plan, man,' said the Man standing up in a hurry.

'We'll he'd better be here soon cuz, or I'm staying. I mean, I'm leaving.'

Three hours went by. I smoked so much dope that I forgot what the Lebanese alphabet looked like.

'Hey, my man, what's the man on about today? Did

you get my text, my man?' asked Tommy from the window.

'Man, my man in a man's outfit. Where did you get those clothes sucker? asked Man.

'Met some heavy dudes in Pitt Street that slap slipped me a beauty. My fashion sense was pushed in big time, my man. Hey, my men Karim and Vince, I heard you went the whole hog and rammed the bank? Did you save a little cash for Tommy?'

He jumped through the window and had a few bongs out of Man's personal stash.

'You got a deal?' asked Karim.

'Hey, my Russian man, you got to slow down, my man, like Mr. Man here and his bible cookbook. He's got the answer to the universe, you know?'

'Bullshit cuz.'

'It's in there somewhere, my man. Man, tell them.'

'It's a secret man. When we were snuggling behind the dumpster, you said you wouldn't tell man.'

'What harm can it do, Mr. Man? We're all rich now, so separate the cash, my man.'

'All of us?' asked Karim.

'Yeah, back door cuz, you didn't help in the robbery, or pack the fucking houses with dope,' I said.

'Neither did you man.'

'Yeah, I know, but neither did he, cuz.'

'Good point essay. So, we should all give the money back then?'

'No, we split the cash three ways.'

'I count four of us here now, my man. And do I need to say you owe me? You left me in the company of strangers, to get hammered by fashion gurus that had firm opinions on what should occur in a change room at closing time. I'm reeling here, my men.'

'So, we need to pay $250K for letting those two lovers bang you?'

'I'm an expensive prospect, my man. All glimmer and royal cheese.'

'Kill him,' said Karim.

'Na man, no violence essays. We can work this out, man. Now Tommy has an idea.'

'Wasn't it your idea, my man?'

'Oh yeah, it was. What was it?'

'It's in the cookbook, page seven.'

'Don't give my secrets away essay. This book is sacred man.'

The man counted the pages until he got to seven.

'Oh yeah man, here it is. Can you read it for me, Tommy?'

'You too stoned my man?'

'Na essay, I can't read.'

The man closed the book and handed it to Tommy. He slowly counted to page seven and read it out loud.

'There is, in waiting, a bag of magic licorice all sorts, that when eaten, give the people magic powers, my man.'

'So?' asked Karim.

'So, we buy the lollies, man, don't you want to get magic powers essay?'

'That's fucking it cuz, I'm dropping you two off back in Pitt Street and we're splitting the money. Give me the money, mate, I'm looking after it. Everyone in the car.'

'I don't have a car, man.'

'Ok in the taxi.'

'Didn't call one man.'

'Then fucking call one! No, Karim, you do it, no! I'll do it.'

An hour later, we were crammed in a taxi on our way to Pitt Street mate. By then, I'd cooled down, so I let Man hold the money. He was smiling the whole time, mate, kissing the briefcase like a sexual deviant.

'Ok, we're stopping for breakfast, mate. I'm starving cuz.'

We pulled over in Pitt Street, just behind the four burnt-out houses. Who the fuck could do such a thing without cleaning up their mess mate. A fucking disgrace, I'm telling ya.

'Where did all the houses come from, my men? You really pulled that off, Vince?'

'It was my idea man. But I'm feeling uneasy essays. We got to hide this money, ay?'

'Yeah, I guess cuz, especially as we're across the street from the bank we robbed.'

'Maybe we can open an account and deposit the

money ay essays? Safe as houses in a bank, man.'

Before we knew it, Man took off with the cash and ran into the Commonwealth Bank, asking to open an account. When we caught up with him, he was talking to the manager.

'Well, thank you, sir, for opening such an important account with us on this wonderful and glorious day. You do realise this is a substantial deposit, and we will need to have it verified by the federal police? I do hope that you understand?'

'Hey man?'

We were all standing behind him.

'Also, there are some privacy issues at hand here, sir. Who are these other gentlemen?'

'Oh yeah, man, I think this is Tommy, Vince, and Karim?'

'And how are these people associated with you?'

'Hey?'

'We're friends cuz.'

'Oh yes, I do believe I saw you and you behind a

dumpster one afternoon. May I ask what you were doing?'

'Oh, my man, we were developing our fashion sense, of course.'

The guy's manager came over.

'Oh, my lord, you beautiful people.'

He started to cry.

'What's wrong sir?'

'These boys have returned our money! Have you counted it, Manny?'

'Yes, Mr. Colistin, exactly one million dollars. But they did say they wanted to open…'

'Oh, forget that, Manny. These boys are heroes. Contact the police and our media department. You guys are going on the newspaper's front page, pronto!'

'Hey?' asked Man.

'You're heroes! Step into my office.'

We talked with the manager and the cops for an hour. We told them we found the money in a dumpster around the corner. Tommy and Man were regulars in that vicinity, so the cops bought the story, mate. After an hour of photos and goodwill, mate, we were all back on the street with a fifty-dollar reward.

'Great idea, cuz, what next, Mr. Man?'

'He's gone, my man,' replied Tommy.

'Where, the dumpster to look for another million mate?'

'I think you hurt his feelings, my man.'

'So, fucking what, the guys a dipshit.'

'Yeah,' said Karim.

'So, where's the money cuz?'

'In my pocket, my man, oh no, sorry, I gave it to Man.'

'Find him, mate.'

'He's over at the dumpster café.'

We walked over and saw a Man with a shopping bag.

'Excuse me, sir, Mr. Man, or whatever your name is, you can't come in here without money. You need to buy something from our establishment.'

Tommy walked over to help.

'He's got $50, my man. Leave him alone.'

'Ok, I'm sorry, it's just that I've seen him at the dumpster so many times it makes my gonads vibrate. Let's see the money then.'

'Show him my man.'

'Hey?'

'The $50 reward.'

Man froze.

'Ok, you'll all need to leave.'

We sat behind the dumpster on Pitt Street whilst cars sped by.

'You spent our only $50 cuz?'

'Yeah man.'

'May I ask on what, mate?'

The man took out four bags of licorice all sorts from a shopping bag and handed them around.

'They're magic man. But only one of them. I don't know which one.'

'You've really fucking lost is ay cuz! And why did it cost $50 for four bags of licorice all sorts?'

'Dunno,' he replied, munching away.

'And how will we know they are magic?'

The man shook his head.

Well, that was it cuz. We left Tommy and Man behind the dumpster and caught a taxi back to Tex's house. We'd have some explaining to do, I'm telling ya mate.

Chapter Ten

'You spent a million dollars on licorice, all sorts? Jesus H fucking Christ. I hope you didn't leave me the black and white ones? I want colour in between my black, you KKK super loving anti-supremist! Now show me the packet. Empty! Not a single one.'

'Ay, Tex, cuz my rawhide beautician. Let's get the story straight, mate. We partnered with two stone heads who liked to bang each other behind a dumpster, then gave back the million because we felt guilty. Then, we got a reward and bought the lollies, cuz. It just so happens that inflation went up by 5600% in a matter of three minutes, and we needed to spend all the reward money. Now, are we all square?'

'Yeah, well, I guess so. A job well done ya beetle juice blood suckers. But after all the shit you've been through, you can't lay a little cash next to me and my larger-than-life AI sex doll?'

'Are you referring to me?' asked Veronica from under the table.

'Well, you know my way of talking sweet love

tangerine, I can't just come out and say the things I feel?'

'But you could say it a bit better than that. I adjust your belt on my knees 20 times a day. A little appreciation, big Tex,' she said, stroking his pants.

'So, what's the plan, cuz?'

'Well, that fella, Mr. Slacker, rang me and said what a good job you did. He wanted to know why you wouldn't rip your kidney out and place it on the table for him. I explained that it was a little beyond your job description, so I think he kidnapped a helicopter pilot and made him give it up instead. But he did say he'd like you to manage his casino that he just bought. This way, you can visit the cash room and get some real dollars. How do you feel about that?'

'In the words of the burning bush at the holy hillside, *what the fuck*?' I asked.

'Don't try to be clever ya preacher mat Pilates look-a-like. I've got more long-winded sayings in my bag of tricks than Captain Cook's starboard sail, so don't fuck with the shit talk meister, you hear?'

I thought I'd seen the face of God, mate.

'I am the face of God, you hear? Now mosey on

down to the casino and ask for Wilfred Jingle, he'll introduce you to Bobby and Tangle. From there, you'll be working with Sally and Thelma, who'll introduce you to my cousin, Eddy. Now go on git now, ya hear.'

'No worries cuz, but how do we get into the cash room, mate?'

'You've got to form relationships, like all those names I just made up before. You understand?'

'Actually, I think I know a Thelma mate.'

'Who works at the casino?'

'Na, I went to school with her on the north shore. Do you think that's her?'

'Unlikely.'

One hour later, we were dropped off at the casino in *Bangthekangaroo*. I think that's what the driver said, but not sure. His voice was all muffled like a mate.

'Are you Mr. Vince?' asked a seven-foot blonde on the steps of the casino.

'Ah, yeah, sure, that's me, cuz. Do we know each other?'

'We do now. My name is Vera. Nice to meet you, Mr. Lombardi.'

'Vera? Really? Isn't that a name that old grannies have because their mothers didn't like them?'

She stared at me for a minute.

'And who is your offsider?'

'Ah, he doesn't talk. I'm much more interesting, mate.'

'But he must have a name?'

'Fucking I dunno, ask him mate.'

'Wow, Mr. Lombardi, you're really good with the ladies.'

'Too right cuz! I'm of the opinion that ladies will automatically warm to my pleasant nature and bulging crotch, and it's not toilet paper, honey, you can be assured of that.'

'I see, may I touch it?'

'What, right here, on the steps?'

'Yes!'

She reached down and undid my fly and pulled out half a roll of toilet paper.

'You were saying, Mr. Lombardi?'

'Ok then, you win, but I'm still packing cuz. Better off than you at the moment, ay? Sexy chick like yourself, all covered in paper waiting to take a shit on the steps.'

She looked up at the sky.

'So perhaps we can start again, Mr. Lombardi. I'm Vera.'

She held out her hand.

'I thought you said Baldrick?'

She walked back up the stairs and talked to some bloke in a grey suit.

'Mr. Lombardi, I don't believe we've had the pleasure? George Styles is my name.'

'You mean pleasure session, mate?'

'Now, Mr. Lomardi, I'm sure Tex has explained that this business is all about relationships. This is a complicated profession. We've got people at us on both sides of the fence. You have to be diplomatic.'

'Like a politician mate?'

'Well, yeah, if you wanna put it that way, like a politician.'

'So why did you have a seven-foot blonde in a red dress called Vara meet me at the steps? Was that diplomatic?'

'Well, being diplomatic is a lot like being manipulative, but we can talk about that later, on my terms and in a manner that I'm happy with. Do you fancy a drink?'

'Will I get to meet Mr. Slacker again?'

'No, I'm sorry, he stole a kidney from a helicopter pilot this afternoon, and he's getting it put in. He'll be out for a week. I heard he asked for yours. Any reason why you didn't hand it over?'

'You are fucking joking, aren't you cuz?'

'No, not really. You see, Mr. Slacker gets what he wants. You are the first man to refuse one of his requests.'

'So, how exactly do I rip a kidney out of my body with my bare hands?'

'I'm not sure on that one, but you refused the great

Mr. Slacker, and he was impressed. He wants you to run his casino until he gets better.'

I was humbled by the guy's smart talk, mate. The words kept coming like he'd read a book and recorded it on a matrix database. Ya know, the one where you plug in and everything's there, mate. I checked the back of his head for a jack mount.

'Excuse me, Mr. Lombardi, why are you touching the back of my head?'

'Have you heard of the Matrix, mate?'

'No.'

'Do you want to know?'

'No.'

'Ok then, so I guess you're not interested in a blue or red pill mate?'

'Look, Mr. Lombardi, please come inside and have a drink. I'll show you around and you can meet all the managers.'

'So, you're a manager?'

'Yes, I'm the assistant manager, sir.'

'And I'm the manager?'

'For now, sir, for now.'

I sat at the bar and ordered a lactose-free chocolate milkshake with cream on top. I wanted one of those glasses they used in the old-style milk bars where the chicks' served hamburgers on roller-skates mate, but they didn't have a fucking clue what I was talking about.

'Ya know, roller skates, short skirts, dudes hanging out of car windows whistling Nat King Cole tunes? Are ya fucking stupid or something?'

'Never heard of him,' said the bar manager.

'Me neither, I was just making it up, impressed?'

'With your manners?'

'No, with my knowledge of history, mate, whatta ya think, yes, my manners. Am I the Trojan horse of the new era, baby?'

'Do I have to work with him, Mr. Styles? I don't like him.'

'That's discrimination, Mr. Styles. She's at me because I'm Lebanese, and because I'm a Muslim, and I pray on a dirty floor, and, and something else, mate.'

'Vince, why are you so hard to get along with? Why don't you take a leaf out of your friend's book here? He looks open-minded, carefree, and easy-going. Where are you from, friend?'

'Russia.'

'Oh, I'm sorry, I'm afraid you we can't be seen together. Please act like we never met.'

This wasn't working mate, and it was all outside of my control. Everyone was against me. But I wasn't about to run back to Tex empty-handed. I wanted into that cash room, and fast.

'Now this is Tina, manager of all that is alcohol and its pleasure effects.'

'I manage the bars, that's enough,' said Tina.

'Alcohol is an integral part of a casino. We aim to relax our customers to the extent where they no longer tick properly and are more than happy to give us their money. When they ask for doubles, we give triples, then direct them to the blackjack tables. We hold ourselves to the highest level of integrity.'

'Shut up Styles, we get em pissed and they blow their cash,' said Tina.

'We form relationships with our biggest gamblers. Do you have any experience behind the bar, Mr. Lombardi?'

'Yeah sure, I once got invited to run a casino and sat with a stiff drinking a milkshake.'

'Very funny, Vince, oh, can I call you Vince?'

'Yeah, cuz.'

'I mean, behind the bar, pouring drinks?'

'Yeah.'

'When?'

'Sometime other than now, why?'

He shook his head.

Five minutes later, I was serving drinks to the high rollers. If they ordered a single, I'd give em triples, just like the head stiff said.

'Hey, bartender, are you trying to poison me, fella?' asked a fat guy in a suit. 'I asked for a straight bourbon whiskey. What is this?'

'It's what you need to help you lose some weight mate.'

'Smells like vodka.'

'It's a mixture, mate: vodka, whiskey, port, sherry, beer, and wine. You got some extras in there, buddy. Ya happy mate?'

'No, because that's not what I ordered.'

'Oh, fuck me till I'm tipsy, look at Mr. *I know fucking everything about alcohol* and the way it's served. Look at you mate, you're fatter than fuck, and you're lecturing me?'

He began to cry, then his girlfriend started on me.

'Can't you see he's sensitive about his weight? What kind of bar are you running here?'

'It's fast and it's furious, mate. It's a Lebbo deck of pure sensation stacked up to your fucking tits love, and that's the way it's going to stay. I'm the new manager love, so love me, or fuck right off.'

The fat fella took a swing at me and hit my shoulder.

'Karim, deck the overeating hippo lover will ya?'

'Busy.'

He was out back, flirting with the cocktail waitresses, banging two at a time. And here I was fighting with a full moon in pure daylight.

'Hey mate, you missed. Turn around so I can see the crack in your ass mate. If you do that and apologise, all will be forgiven.'

'Fuck you Lebbo boy, I'm outa here.'

He walked towards the entrance.

'Hey fat cunt, the betting tables are over there, mate!'

The fella walked straight out, spitting on the ground. Luckily, he left his wallet on the bar, so I grabbed the cash and put it in the till to show everyone what a nice guy I was. Pretty soon after, Styles returned with Tina to get a progress report.

'Fantastic, cuz, the till is full and the booze is flowing mate. Got it under control cuz.'

'That's great, Vince, would you like to see the kitchen?'

'Sure mate, what can Karim do?'

'Take coats at the door, there's a nice lad.'

'Eat my sickle,' replied Karim.

The kitchen was my safe place, mate. There was nothing that I couldn't cook that didn't taste like tabouleh salad, or something with tabouleh in it. I was on the watch for any chef who looked anti-salad mate, or who stared at me sideways when I brushed up against them and spat in their ear. The dishes needed to be perfect mate, like a perfect set of tits at midnight. I wanted that kitchen to run like a well-oiled Lebbo mama, and within an hour, I'd cleared the room.

'Hey dickheads, the food won't cook itself! Get back in here!'

They were fucking cowards' mate, all of them. So, I decided to cook a massive Tabouleh salad and bring it out in a giant bowl for everyone. I ignored any orders that didn't have what I was cooking and just went for it, mate. I needed some help, so Karim came in and helped for a while.

'Fucking stiff, I kill him,' yelled Karim.

'Karim, go get the Bulgur.'

'Vulgar?'

'Na, Bulgar, cracked wheat mate. It's the heart of a

tabouleh salad, cuz.'

Karim brought some raw wheat out of the cool room and smashed it with a meat cleaver.

'What is that, mate?' I asked.

'Cracked wheat.'

'Are you sure? Looks different.'

'I dunno.'

'Yeah? Well, I guess. Looks different though, ay?'

I chopped up some old parsley, mint, thirty onions, one cucumber, sixty cloves of garlic, and soaked it all in chicken juice that was just sitting there under five kilos of old drumsticks. And when I rolled it out in a giant bowl, everyone lined up at the table.

'Ay dickheads, wrong table mate, that's the gelato line. This is real Lebbo tabouleh mate, invented in the bosom of a fat ugly chick who wears black all day and smells like roadkill. Get over here ya chicken shit assholes. It's free, ya know, ay hang on, no it's twenty bucks a bowl.'

'So, how are you going, Vince? asked Styles.

'Fuck mate, don't creep up on me like that. What's

your problem?'

'No problem, what's that you're serving, oh let me guess, tabouleh salad from the bosom of Lebbo land?'

'You've got ESP powers ya stiff prick. How'd ya know mate?'

'We have cameras in the kitchen. Actually, we were watching the Russian for communist behaviour.'

'What's that look like?'

'Well, you know, waiting in the corner to report to a supervisor who is supervised by another and yet another until anyone and everyone knows what you ate for breakfast 16 years ago to the day. You know, stuff like that.'

'Oh, ok, he was just helping with the salad.'

'Smashing idea, Vince, did he make any phone calls using a two-way radio by any chance?'

Karim picked up his fork. He was ready to kill.

'How about rigged an election so the same person wins fifty years in a row?'

'In the kitchen?'

'How about standing opposite a burning bush,

planning the destruction of all mankind?'

'Now you're being a smart-ass mate.'

'Well, you can't be too careful these days, can you? I'm just being a team player, you see, one for all and all for us, you know how it is?'

'Shut up and try the salad you streak of pelican shit.'

The only people who tried the salad were two elderly Lebbo ladies who said God was on their side. They kept screaming God's name whilst they ate at the table. After a mouthful each, they chucked in a mop bucket.

'I can't understand it, Karim. It's an age-old recipe, mate. Maybe I need to cook the wheat next time?'

'One tablespoon of vodka, and a couple of days, all good.'

'So, vodka fixes everything, mate?'

'Here come stiff again.'

Styles walked in holding up a piece of paper.

'Mr. Lombardi, we've had an official complaint about you.'

'Na, it wasn't me mate, the other kid took my lunch box first, cuz. I was just hiding it in the closet for a bit. I didn't know his father's ashes were in there.'

'No, this is about the man at the bar that you insulted.'

'Any witnesses?'

'Yes, there was a young lady.'

'Any other witnesses?'

'No.'

'You see, mate, only one credible witness and a fat piece of lard. That's not enough to hold up in court, cuz.'

'This is not a legal matter, Vince.'

'Ok then, good, let me know when the cops get here, otherwise show me the blackjack tables. Karim, let's go.'

I was on the back foot with the stiff from then on. Everywhere I went he was looking at me cuz, like I was gonna fuck up everything that he'd ever created in his short pitiful existence mate. Too fucking self-conscious in my opinion.

I sat down with Karim at a blackjack table and

introduced myself. The guy was so short he could only just see over the counter.

'Are you the guy from the funeral home, mate?'

'No sir.'

'Are you sure? A midget works there and says stupid stuff all the time.'

'I'm not a midget sir.'

'Are you sure? Have you been professionally diagnosed?'

'No, sir, I haven't.'

'Then how do you fucking know mate? Ok hit me!'

'With what sir? My hand?'

Karim laughed.

'Isn't that what you say at these places, mate?'

The stiff stepped in.

'Excuse me, Vladimir, Mr. Lombardi is our new manager until Mr. Slacker's kidney heals. He's still learning how to act in these places.'

'Fuck off, mate. Don't talk to me for the rest of the day.'

Styles walked off in a huff.

'Now hit me?'

'I haven't dealt yet, sir.'

'Then fucking double hit me.'

He dealt me a two of diamonds and gave himself a king of hearts.

'That's not fair, mate. Start again.'

'I'm sorry, sir, that's not allowed.'

'Alright then, I'm changing tables.'

I went from table to table until I got the card I wanted – the illustrious ace of spades.

'Finally, cuz, and you got the two of hearts ya poor bastard, now hit me!'

'Two of spades sir.'

'Ah fuck this, I'm changing tables.'

By this time my ass was getting sore, and it wasn't due to a quick visit behind the dumpster.

'Ay? You again? Haven't you knocked off?'

'We only talked ten minutes ago, sir. Would you like a card?' said the midget.

'Yeah, maybe, I wanna pick.'

'I'm sorry, sir, that's not allowed.'

'I wanna use my own cards.'

'I'm sorry …'

'I'm sorry, I'm sorry! Is that all you can fucking say? If you had any heart, you'd be out looking for your Mama, cooking something nice for her in her old age.'

'I'm an orphan sir.'

'Stop making fucking excuses, now hit me!'

He took a swing and missed.

'You're fired mate, get the fuck out! Karim, take his place.'

I went to the toilet, thinking the stiff would be in there tugging on his pink gluten free wiener, but I had the place to myself, so I took a well deserve shit. Seemed like I was in there forever cuz, because when I returned, there was a crowd around Karim's blackjack table with piles of chips lined up in front of each player mate.

'What's up Karim? Are we winning?' I asked at the back of the table.

'Yes.'

'I mean us, not them.'

'What difference?'

I stood beside Karim for a few seconds and realised he was giving out cards on request. If a player asked for the king of hearts, Karim would sort through the pack and hand it out, mate.

'Um, Karim, I don't think this is the way the game is played, mate?'

'Sorry.'

The midget came back and tapped Karim on the shoulder. He had to jump.

'What?'

'He tapped him again.'

'What, piss off! You want job back?' asked Karim.

'Yes, please, sir. Mr. Styles would like to talk with you both in his office.'

'No way, mate. He just wants a pleasure session. All these exec types are the same cuz, stand up citizens by day, then they bang the crap out of anything that moves when the doors are shut. Tell him to fuck right off!'

The crowd cheered.

'We're going over to the slot machines anyway, cuz. You stay here and be Mr. Perfect midget. And by the way, we've changed the rules. The players can now ask for any card they want, but you can't, is that clear?'

'Yes, sir.'

When I walked away, he said something under his breath. Sounded like *mutter trucker* or something similar.

The slot machines were my favourite, mate. Those spinning green and yellow things stopped me in my tracks. The whole thing was one huge hypnotic Babylonian wonderland. I was swaying on my feet just looking at all the rhinestone cowboys, sitting on their own special chairs, with cushioned seating and little fucking place mats to put their drinks on. I was jealous.

'Hey Karim? Get me the stiff. I've got a complaint, mate.'

'He in office.'

'Ah yeah right, well then you listen. Tell me why these people get luxurious accommodation if they're losers?'

'Not know.'

'Well, of course you don't know. If I don't know, then why would you?'

I'd confused him.

'Ok, I'm gonna make some changes. These little twirly things need to slow down a little. I can't see which way they're turning and what's written on them.'

'Can see now, look it say BAR,' said Karim.

'I know, idiot, but I want to see it when it's spinning, is that too much to ask?'

'And then?'

'And then when the BAR comes around, I push stop, then I can get three in a row. So, how do you slow these things down?'

'Dunno.'

'Then be useful and go and get me a screwdriver, will ya?'

He reached into his crotch and pulled out a Phillips head screwdriver.

'You perverted maniac, what's this?'

'Better than toilet paper.'

'Ha, you're turning into a smart ass cuz, moving up in the world mate.'

I closed down the whole poker machine section and worked on them, mate. I unscrewed anything that had screws and asked Karim to remember the order I undid everything.

'Ok done, now which part do I put back first, cuz?'

'What?'

'The order, mate, I asked you to watch.'

'I order fish and chips, you hungry?'

'Yeah, I guess so mate.'

I was over getting angry at the fella. I just wanted him to find his mother and settle down.

With the poker machines in bits, we decided to seek out the cash room before Styles caught up with us. He was on the prowl cuz, pacing up and down in his special little fucking office on the top floor. The guy had glass panel walls so everyone on the gambling floor could see what he was doing. I reckon I saw him holding someone's head under the table at one stage.

'Is this the cash room?' I asked the cashier.

'I'm sorry, sir, not even cashiers are allowed in the cash room?'

'So, let me in on your little secret here, cuz, if cashiers don't handle cash, what exactly what do they do, mate?'

'We take the cash to the cash room where the head cashiers count it.'

'Ah, I see, so I should be talking to a head cashier mate, is that all I need to do?'

'Not exactly, you need to get a pass from a cashier to enter the cash room. Then you will have to show that pass and ID when you knock on the door. If the head cashier like the handwriting on the paper, and your breath doesn't smell like dog food, you will be given the chance to enter.'

'What? Are you fucking insane cuz? How am I supposed to remember that, mate? Anyway, I'm the manager. I'm going in.'

We entered the cash room through an open door. The senior head cashier went to take a piss and left the door open.

'Excuse me, sir, what are you doing in the cash room? Only senior cashiers are allowed?' said a tall, thin man in a 1980s suit.

'You left the door open ya dumb shit.'

'Now look, you grubby man, you grubby grubby little man. I am entrusted to take care of this institution, Mr. Speaker. This room has personal and sensitive information that pertains to all but a few people. The Australian population has thrusted that task on my shoulders, and I will not let them down!'

'Why did he say Mr. Speaker cuz? And why is he turning in circles when he talks, mate?' I asked Karim.

'Well, it's simple, Mr. Speaker, you need to leave before the next census date, or low and behold, I will call a referendum of the people, and they will speak loudly, Mr. Speaker, and the world will listen once more to the highest class in the land, the senior cashier and all that lies before him.'

'What fucking planet are you living on mate? You've got your head up your ass.'

'My planet.'

'So can I stay?'

He paused.

'Yeah, I guess so, if you be my friend.'

'Why, mate?'

'Because I don't have any.'

'So, who's this Mr. Speaker mate?'

'He's my imaginary friend. I like him because he never calls me out on anything. I can basically say anything I want, and the dumb shit just says things like 'I call you to order', and 'will you please', and 'the member for whoever and whatever.' He's a nice bloke though.'

'And this happens in a casino, mate?'

'Well, not exactly.'

'So, show me how this all works then, stiff cuz.'

'You can call me Saul Beating.'

'Is that your name?'

'No, it's someone else's! Don't make me swear in the House of Parliament.'

This guy was entertaining, mate.

'So, you see the conveyer belt and the coins that roll about on both sides of the house?'

'Yeah mate.'

'Well, it goes around this part of the belt, like a toy train on a track, similar to Thomas and the fat controller, and how he managed the situation so well without being told what to do. Then it drops into a box, and when it's full, we call the cash trans guys, and it all starts again.'

'You mean the guys who pick it up are transsexuals' mate?'

'Of course, that's what I mean! No, they're transport security guards that take the money to the bank, you outgoing member with an agenda. Come back at lunch time and I'll have a shipment ready for you. Knock on the door and I'll open the chamber.'

This guy was weird, mate. I hated his creepy suits and the way he stood over you and breathed out yesterday's sandwiches. I could see all the lettuce and bread stuck between his teeth, mate.

We arrived back at the cashier office smack bang on the lunch break.

'Knock on the door, cuz,' I asked Karim.

'How many times?'

'Um, three mate.'

'Why three?'

I knocked on the door.

'What the hell are you doing? Don't you come around here banging on the door like some kind of cop, have some respect for the ones who make the ultimate sacrifice and outlay their talents and skills for the everyday citizen.'

'Ok mate, whatever you say. You got the money mother fucker?'

'Yes, take those foir boxes to the bank. When you get there ask for Rob Dork, I worked with him for many years and we've literally taken turns to fuck the country. He'll explain when you get there, but only if you ask him to.'

'Great, Karim, grab the boxes.'

Four boxes of coins were pretty heavy cuz. Lucky Karim had a strong right arm, mate. All that tugging with Mrs. Palm and her five sons had paid off.

Half an hour later, we were in the car pretending to drink Champagne. We had the goods, and we were on the way to Tex's place to count the loot. He'd be proud for sure.

'So finally, you boys have brought home the paper-loving system that keeps the trees watered and the cows fed. Let's count the money and see what ya got?'

Tex got out his money-counting machine.

'Na cuz, it's all coins mate, fucking heavy as well.'

'Veronica, can you please bring the coin counting machine?'

'Well, that's better, my love, you're finally showing some respect to your number one toy pony. You know I like you more when you say honey bun words, makes me want to look after your sizzling steak sausage with extra lard.'

Fucking hell mate, this chick was hooked on American grain fed beef.

'So how many boxes?' asked Tex.

'Four,' said Karim.

'Ok then, take 'em out, let's get all the coins out of their holders.'

It took an hour to break the coins free from the paper casing. There were so many fucking coins, we could've started our own bank mate.

'Ok, put 'em in, can you count 'em out loud, sugar

britches?'

'Why sure, daddy long middle leg. It's my pleasure.'

'So that's four boxes, 27,900 coins divided by 100 is $279.'

'What the *tornado red slipper thief* are you talking about? There are four boxes full of money there, my steamed sweet love potato.'

'And they're all one-cent pieces, my love canal mechanic. It's counted right and proper.'

'Jesus, fix the fence with bubble gum, you stupid bastards only grabbed the one-cent coins?'

'It was Saul Beating, he talked so much about saving the world and abusing it at the same time, so we got distracted.'

'Alright then, I'm taking $275 of this money and handing back $4. That'll get you into the local pool and buy something to eat. And there are no BBQs there, so don't be asking for Texas T-bone or grain-fed marble steaks, ok?'

'What are you talking about, cuz?'

'I haven't finished with you jelly-fed tyrants. You're

going to work in an aquatic centre. Ask for Mrs. Havisham.'

Shit mate, an actual swimming pool cuz? The closest I got to one back in Lebanon was a two-kilometre deep well with mildew on the walls. And the thing is, I reckon I knew Mrs. Havisham from my days on the north shore, cuz.

Chapter Eleven

I had a skip in my step when we reached Marrickville Aquatic Centre, but Karim was getting lazy on me mate, so I turned around and had a go at him.

'Get that lip off the ground, cuz. We're going to a swimming pool, mate. Diving boards, water slides, bikini-clad teenagers, what's the problem?'

'I can't swim.'

'Oh yeah, neither can I. Don't worry about it, mate. Did Jesus sack all of his disciples for having dinner on one side of a table? Did Neil Armstrong push his mates out the way because he needed to take a piss outside?'

'Hey?'

'The point is we can do it, mate.'

'How?'

'We'll swim at the shallow end.'

'You really know lady in pool?' asked Karim.

'Yeah, I think so mate. That means we're in cuz. Let me do the talking.'

'Mrs. Have-a-shag, how are you, dear? You look better than ever, my love. You've had a lip resurgence, a skin fracture, and a hair transplant,' I said in front of the pool tuck shop.

'Lombardi!' she replied.

'May I call you Mrs. H for short?'

'Get out! The last time I saw you, I gave you and your Nicaraguan girlfriend a life ban.'

'I don't remember that. You've got such a good memory, Mrs. H, that's incredible.'

'Oh, do you think so?'

'Oh yes, I really do mean it, madam. Look into the mirror beside you Mrs. H. You are living perfection my dear; a love doll that's been given the rank of specimen try out for Hulk Hogan, an angel that's fallen to earth after eating too much, or a painting of a Nazi Germany bunker.'

'Shut up, Lombardi! It's been twenty years so I guess I can give you one more chance, but if you even fucking move, I'll kick you and your Russian toy boy out the door, got it?'

'You mean I can't move from this spot?'

She picked up a broomstick and whirled it around her head. Her tuck shop underarms were hypnotic, mate, all wobbly like Aeroplane jelly set by grandma in that extra special loving way.

'That's one dollar entry fee,' she said.

'Hey, it was only 50 cents last time, mate. How can you justify the inflation, cuz?'

'That was twenty years ago, and I don't need to justify anything! Now, Tex said you two wanted to be lifeguards, am I correct?'

'Yeah, I guess so cuz. What did you have in mind?' I said slowly.

'Being a lifeguard.'

'Oh yeah.'

'You two got your Bronze Medallion, CPR, and all the bells and whistles?'

I wiggled my Lebbo snake down below and heard a jingle.

'Yeah, sure, Mrs. H. All good down there.'

'Well, get up on those chairs and keep a lookout, and if I catch you two perving on the teenage girls, I'll suffocate you inside my fat rolls, see!'

She flipped up her dress and unveiled her magnificent whale bumps. Starvation survival to some, a lethal weapon to others. She was packing in every regard, mate, and all the while, her daughter Gertrude was bobbing in and out from behind her, like a gopher looking for angry golfers.

'Here, take these dark sunglasses, you'll need them, mate.'

'Why?' asked Karim.

'Because it's glary mate, that's all.'

We sat up on those highchairs looking at the action, mate. I tried to be like a grown-up, but people kept looking at me, expecting the opposite. I came down a few times and confronted the crowd, asking 'what are ya looking at, cuz?' But they just shrugged their shoulders and lied straight to my face, mate.

'Hey Karim, check that kid out, mate. Is she alright?'

A daddy's nightmare bikini-clad influencer was

passed out on the lawn. Mrs. H came running over and cleared the crowd.

'Lombardi, get down here?'

'Yeah, ok mate, don't make a scene for Christ's sake, cuz, I'm coming.'

When I got there, I made a professional decision to give mouth-to-mouth resuscitation.

'You've got your CPR, right?' she asked me.

'Yeah sure, Mrs. H, I can blow air into a star-struck hippo in outer space. Step back my formidable hump whale.'

She went to slap me.

'Think about the girl, Mrs. H, do what's right. Hmmm?'

She managed to get those troll feet of hers in reverse.

'You'll keep Lombardi, now blow!'

'My pleasure!'

When I leant over the top of the star struck teenager, she opened her eyes a little.

'This girl has sunstroke, hold this towel over her face, Karim.'

I latched onto her love lips and began to blow mate. My tongue may have slipped in a few times and performed the ancient art of karma wiggle, but I just can't remember. When she came too, she dobbed me into the resident bullfrog, but I just said she was delirious, and needed to go to the hospital. Patient cured cuz!

'Take a break, I'm hungry,' said Karim.

'We've still got a dollar. Let's get a bag of mixed lollies, mate.'

We walked over to the tuck shop and asked Gertrude for two bags.

'Here,' she said, plodding them onto the counter.

'How many in each one, cuz?'

'Mum said you used to ask that question all the time. She said if you ask it again, then I should go and get her.'

'And then what, mate?'

'And then I'll have told her and she'll be here, so there!'

'You half-baked little shit, do you know who you're messing with little girl? We're with Tex mate, and he's a bad ass cuz.'

'You and your cowboy Roy Rogers timeline fuckup doesn't scare me. I've got Mum on my side, and she's tougher than all your nostalgic black and white posters.'

She was fucking good cuz. Only 12 years old and her shit talk was fully developed mate.

'So, you won't tell me, mate?'

'I dunno, I think there's 20 or so in each bag?'

'Did you bag them up, cuz?'

'Yeah.'

'So, how many?'

'In each bag?'

'Yes, in each fucking bag you idiot! Now tell me!'

She started crying, screaming for her Mum.

'Shit, Karim grab all the bags of lollies, and we'll count them over there mate.'

We took around fifty bags and emptied them on the concrete next to the pool.

'Now don't mix them all together, or we won't know how many are in each bag, ok, cuz? I've gotta take a piss.'

When I came back, the lollies were all in a pile.

'What did I say, Karim! Not altogether, didn't you hear me, mate?'

'It's ok, we bag up again. 20 in each bag. It fair.'

'What are all the wriggly things in the pile, mate?'

'I think ant, but ok, we bag.'

'And what's that smell, that fucking horrid smell mate?'

'I dunno.'

'Bullshit, did you take a shit on the grass mate?'

'I may have, but I just can't remember. I learn that sentence from you.'

'Yeah, you're getting better cuz, that's for sure, but we can't bag up here sitting next to your shit, let's find another place.'

'Throw them in pool.'

'Why, mate?'

'Chlorine, and sugar, making for good digestion. I learn this from a book.'

'From a book, mate?'

'I learn, from a book.'

'Bullshit cuz, you're having me on mate, fucking with me brain ya clear spirits director, aren't you?'

'Yes.'

By that time, Mrs. H was standing over us with hands on her hips.

'Who shat in the pool?'

'Ha?' I answered.

'There's a log in the pool, and everyone is saying it was you. Now no one is swimming, and one of you is to blame.'

'Fuck off, mate!'

I felt the hand of Allah grab me by the back of my jocks and hurl me out onto the street. It was like divine intervention, cuz. I looked back and saw Karim standing by the pool entrance, eating a Polly Waffle. Everyone thought it was the shit he laid and passed out, but Gertrude wasn't fooled.

'I know it's only a Polly Waffle, you can't fool me you pair of public-school fuckups. I hope Tex shaves your ass and teaches you to walk backwards. Now don't come back here again, or I'll hypnotize you, and tell your subconscious that you're a bad person.'

We walked down the road and hailed a taxi in our underwear.

Chapter Twelve

'Well, if it isn't walking evidence that fuckups don't die a young death. Get over here you two and sit you asses down on my three-inch shag carpet,' said Tex.

'We can't sit on a chair cuz?'

'Please yourself.'

We felt like school kids in trouble, and Veronica wasn't anywhere to be seen, mate.

'So how did it go?'

'Fucking awesome cuz, real intelligent and professional development ay? I learnt how to spell chlorine.'

'Ok, spell it then,' asked Tex.

There was a long silence.

'Ok then, I heard some good things about your casino escapade that make me believe you can succeed in the restaurant business. Did you make the gelato that everyone was raving about the other night?' asked Tex.

'Aw, yeah, cuz, that was my food line ay. Some other dude was serving some kind of salad, and it didn't go too well. Felt sorry for him cuz.'

'Well, before I drop you off at your mother's house, I want you to organise a party for me at the local pub. I'm inviting guests from all over, so the food needs to be a world-class superpower with tariff exemptions, ya hear?'

Me and Karim looked at each other.

'We're getting tired captain America, ya know, we're fucked, rooted, sleepy, dazed…'

'Yeah, I catch your drift. Don't worry, there'll be something in it for you two. I'm not one to take all the attention from others when there's a conference, except for every global convention known to man, United Nations meetings, and anything to do with someone else's business. Other than that, I'm all for giving and not receiving. Can you handle it kid?'

'You mean, I get to see mum again?' I asked.

'Too right, cowboy, and I may have a present for your cowgirl as well?'

'I don't have a girlfriend, mate.'

'I was talking about Karim, now git over to the pub and sort it out.'

'Which one cuz?'

'The one in Surrey Hills. You can't miss it, it's the one on the corner with no parking, and the bartenders stare at you to evaluate your class and gender when you walk in. Got it?'

'Yeah, cuz, sure mate.'

'We good,' said Karim.

'Geez cuz, how fucking exciting ay? He's got a surprise for you, mate. See, what did I tell ya, stick with me and I'll take ya places ay?'

'Where?'

'Here mate, right fucking here. I think it's time for a little celebration cuz, a right piss up party I reckon. Let's go to Woolworths and buy all the shit for the party mate. You still got those vouchers you stole from a letterbox in Marrickville?'

'Yeah.'

We ran down to Woollies, grabbed $50 worth of breakfast sausages, and ran out of the fire escape, mate. The vouchers we had were out of date, so I didn't see any need to embarrass Karim at the checkout.

When we got to the pub in Surry Hills, it was full of men in shorts and t-shirts. It looked like they'd been working out every day of their lives, ready for someone to throw them a rugby ball and say, go fetch, boy, cuz! There were panthers, roosters, and many other animals on their shirts, mate, so I assumed they all worked in a zoo.

'Hey, zoo people, knocking bag a few cold ones, ay cuz? Fancy a mixed lolly? I think I've still got a couple.'

I reached down my pants a brought out a crinkled bag of mixed lollies and offered them around. Not a single taker, mate. I was pissed.

'You fucking snobs' mate. I come downtown and offer my lollies from the bosom of Babylon, and you knock me back, well that's really fucking nice of you, ay?'

'Excuse me, sir, you can't bring all those sausages in here. This is a front bar, sir,' said the lady cuz behind the bar.

Me and Karim were loaded with wholesome breakfast sausages, mate. I remember eating those things as a kid. I'd eat seven or eight, then chuck in the toilet. Mum said it was the supermarket trying to poison immigrants by employing nasty trauma-ridden butchers who laced them with fat, and more fat, fat extract, and gluten-free lard mate. These sausages are so fucking fat, they add a quarter pound of blubber to a quarter pounder burger at McDonalds.

'Hey, that's discrimination against non-Australians, mate. You wouldn't say that to these rugby monkeys. All they can do is run with a ball and say, yay! I know your type, mate, so be careful or I'll get my 275 cousins onto you,' I said to the bar babe.

'I'm sure you're exaggerating, sir. Now you'll have to leave.'

'From where, mate?'

'Here sir.'

'See, there you go again, discriminating against boat people. Do you know how fucking long I sat next to this prick beside me? Do ya? He farted like a mad man and swore like a president invading a nearby country because it was nearby. Have a little heart, babe.'

Karim nodded.

'Excuse me, sir, exactly what are you going to do with those sausages anyway?'

'Cook em, mate.'

'In a front bar?'

'Yeah sure, just wheel out the flat top BBQ and we'll fire it up next to the jukebox mate. These 100m sprint perfectionists won't mind.'

'Sorry, who sent you two here?'

'Tex mate, the one and only 52 star-spangled delight, the American dream fraudster, the alligator wrestler, the …'

'Yes, sorry, sir, we know him.'

'So can I cook the sausages or not, mate?'

I looked around at all the men in tight shorts. They looked kinda pissed off and were acting weird. I could see roosters, rabbits, and panthers all around me. We were surrounded, so I needed the lady cuz to stick up for me.

'Don't expect me to stick up for you,' said the lady cuz.

Karim took out a hammer and sickle from his pants and cried out something in Russian.

'Where've you been keeping those, mate?'

'Down pants.'

'I can see that, mate.'

'Did Tex make a booking, bar babe?'

'Let me see, yes, you're in function room number three, but you'll need to cook those sausages outside. You can leave the coleslaw behind the bar.'

'Hey, Karim, where'd you get that salad mate?'

'Woollies' dumpster. I said hello to Tommy.'

'I see you have other guests arriving soon. Would you like me to show them in when they get here?'

'Yes, thanks bar babe, that's what I like from the Australian community, a little fucking respect when respect is due cuz. You get me fellas? And why do you name all your teams after animals? Does that mean you're animals too?'

A huge Polynesian guy towered over us. He was seven feet tall and must have weighed 180kg. He looked uneducated, mean, and nasty. I instantly took a likening to him, mate.

'Hey, c'mon little fella. Surely, we can work this out in an amicable manner. We're all on this boat together, so let's all sing a song of mutual respect and hug,' he said.

I instantly took a disliking to the guy after previously liking him.

'Karim, take him to the Woolies dumpster and introduce him to Tommy, will ya, cuz?'

He gave him directions out front, and the guy took off, hopping down the middle of the road. One bloke said he was the captain of the Rabbitohs club. He was in character, mate, that's for sure.

'Ok then, lady bar cuz, thanks for looking after us, and sorry we didn't come at topless hour. We'll be back with a magnifying glass.'

We lit up the flat burner and started cooking out back. There was traffic everywhere, but we could see the guests arrive, one after the other, mate. Tex was the first to walk inside.

'Jesus, if it ain't the football impersonators of the 21st century. Don't you know that you boys are not entirely the real deal? For starters, where's your fucking armor? And that ball is too big. Can you fellas please get with the fucking program? Did I hear a sorry Tex?'

The boys looked at the bar babe.

'So, you must be Tex, sir?'

'That's me bar babe? Do you mind if I call you that? And why aren't you topless?'

'No comment sir. You can go through to function room number three.'

'I wanted number 52, after all the stars on our god like flag.'

'We only have three function rooms, sir.'

'Yeah, well, I guess I can let you off. But you boys, I'll be watching you.'

Veronica was next to arrive.

'Did Tex come through Alicia?' she asked.

'Yeah, he's out back.'

'How's the topless industry treating you?'

'Oh, I don't do that anymore. Just a regular bar girl doing bar girl things, ya know?'

'Yeh Alicia, gimmy a flash babe?' said the Panthers' head coach.

'No way, Tommy, well, maybe later, after 6 pm.'

The whole team smiled.

'Can I can go through then?' asked Veronica.

'Yeah, sure, honey.'

'Great, I'll be back at 6 pm then.'

Now that Tex had his chief belt adjuster by his side, it was Buster and Limmy's turn to steal the show.

'Cum fuk love doo,' said Limmy, looking around the joint.

'Eh Eshays, don't worry about Limmy adlays, He's just being friendly.'

'Cum tucker mother fucker,' he said with his thumbs snapping his suspenders.

'You boys from around here?' asked a thick-set fella.

'Tom shit up ya, pig snot crap log.'

'Ok, sorry bro, just asking mate.'

Anything said to Limmy other than hello was a personal insult.

'Is that a meat cleaver down your pants, sir?' asked Alicia.

He quickly adjusted his pants, so the handle stuck out first.

'Ok, well, I'll see you at 6 pm as well, I guess.'

'Clever do do.'

As soon as Limmy and Buster went through, Alicia shut the front door and put up a sign. *Access to function room three is around the back.*

When everyone arrived, they sat down at the round table and introduced themselves. The room had a shit load of personality mate.

'Jesus Christ, I don't believe it, all you varmints actually showed up. I thank you from the front page of the bible to the back. Now, where's that food I've been hearing about?'

'Surprise dickheads!'

I kicked open the door and plonked 350 burnt breakfast sausages and twenty tubs of hot coleslaw on the table.

'No knives and forks, ladies, just hoe in with your bare hands. Don't be scared, c'mon now.'

'Now listen, deary, you haven't learnt any manners since we last met, have you? And where is Mr. Converter these days? He was a top-class involuntary performer, I do say. Is he coming deary? He owes me for the milk he drank from my fridge,' said Granny.

'Shut up you asshole dung beetle, you got three days with Mr. Converter tied to a bed, that's $10,000 of free bed barning for nothing. That's good value, you hear?' said Tex.

'Hey gringo, don't be too hard on the old bugger ay? She's looking for a stone-cool breeze in midsummer. I'll keep her happy if you wanna let her go,' said Pablo.

'All yours, Coke head,' replied Tex.

'Well, I'd like to say that observations like these make me believe that going to university is a waste of time. I've read a thousand books in my damp study at the hospital, and nothing compares to the wisdom in this room. If I were to take leave without pay, I'd certainly visit any one of you and bring a scribe to take notes,' said Brains.

'Ok whatever, and did you finish cleaning up that vodka shit mate?'

'All in a day's work, my ripe livered friend. Fancy a

stroll by the dumpster later, I hear Tommy is in need.'

'What'd ya do to him cuz? He's harmless, mate.'

'Oh yes indeed, and his spleen was as tasty as a hyena's hide dried in the sun. But now I'm after a new subject, one that can satisfy my tastes, in and out of bed, you see.'

'Anyone at this table qualify, mate?'

'You catch on fast, my sausage friend. Tell me, did you burn those sausages by accident, or are you sending us a message, one of destruction, or liberation in this conformed society?'

'God damn it Brains, this is a preacher porn loving party. You can't relax for a minute?' asked Tex.

'I'll try Texas Ranger, I'll try.'

Listening to Brains speak was like watching old people fuck. He took his time and made long-winded sentences that came out too slow, mate. Smart fucker though.

'Well, I'd like to say something, Mr. Texas, if that's alright. Is the floor clear?' asked Saul Beating.

'Well, I dunno, I haven't looked down there yet. Any

reason why I should?'

'Now I'd like to point out one thing, Mr. Speaker: there is an abundance of personalities in this room that could one day rule the majority of people in this country. I see so much diversity that it could possibly be the most important moment in my life. But before I go into that, let me say this: when I was a young boy, I liked to go swimming in the river, and that river was so deep, my mother made me wear a life jacket. I hated my mother for that, and she never apologized for doing it either. Now, back to democracy and all that it entails.'

'Will you shut up, Saul? I told you at the swimming pool all those years ago that no one wants to hear it. Everyone is equal in the eyes of a tuck shop tyrant, so stop with the chlorine shit will ya?' said Mrs. Havisham.

'Well, it's easy for some who can wake up in the morning and roll over onto another roll which was resting on two more rolls of lard. You, my dear, need a lesson in democracy and free banter exchange,' replied Saul.

'Perhaps you can visit my humble establishment in the bosom of our local hospital, Mrs. Havisham. I'm always looking to make good stock,' said Brains.

'Hey, leave the lady cuz alone, mate. She's almost crying, mate.'

Mrs. Havisham left in tears. It took a political streak of pelican shit, and a ski masked pool noddle hoarder to fuck it up for everyone.

'Boss, the dame boss, the dame,' said Ponto.

In walked Alicia with a cake.

'Oh, Ponto, why do you get so excited when someone of the opposite sex walks into the room? Is it 6 pm yet?' asked Cedric.

'Why?' asked Alicia.

'Oh, no reason, my dear, someone just said that 6 pm was a good time to pop by. No matter.'

'That cake looks good, Budda, can you buy something like that at Centrelink?' asked Jimmy.

'Oh my god, what a question to ask at such an important time, oh my god, what is the world coming to, and what happened to Tommy? Mr. Brains, did you eat him after I did? What's left behind the dumpster, you crude man?' asked Mario.

'Don't worry about Tommy, ok mate, he's fine cuz.

Bar babe has brought out the cake, so let's just eat, mate.'

'Hold the red coats from eating the blue ones. There are 4.75 more guests to come, and I do believe they're here now,' said Tex.

'4.75?' asked Veronica.

There was a knock at the back door.

'C'mon in ya lily livered party newcomers,' said Tex in his best voice.

Two old ladies and three kids walked in. The last one was really small, mate.

'Let me introduce the one and only Mrs. Lombardi, Mrs. Ivanov, and the three young ones,' said Tex.

We stood there frozen.

'Mutter?' asked Karim.

'Mama?' I asked.

'Oh my god, I'm gonna cry, oh my god, can I use the tablecloth?' asked Mario.

'Fit for a stainless-steel dish, I do believe,' said Brains.

Me and Karim ran over with wild cat smiles and hard peckers, but tripped over the thick shag carpet and landed at their feet.

'You help?' asked Mutter Ivanov.

'You mean I help you or you help me, cuz?'

Karim began to cry.

'We help each other.'

And we did. There were hugs all round, and the three kids joined in. It was like this love fest for those who were only interested in love and all the bullshit that came with it. Saul Beating got up to speak about the moment, but someone threw a burnt sausage at him.

'Hey, mama, cuz, where are my 275 cousins, mate? Are they back at the house?'

'No, they here. Can't you see my boy? This is Rami and Effie, but Dimmy is a little short, so we call 0.75.'

'0.75 mate. That's his nickname? You couldn't think of anything better than that?'

'Don't be smart-ass!'

'But mama, that's still not 275, mate.'

'Who said that?'

'I did, mate.'

'No, it 2.75, not 275, you get?'

I thought it was farfetched, but it was a fucking good yarn to lay on the people, ay cuz?

About The Author

A Bold New Voice in Fiction, Paul Drewitt writes fearless, fast-paced stories packed with wit, grit, and unforgettable characters. With a talent for dark humor and sharp satire, he's quickly becoming a must-read author for fans of edgy, impactful storytelling.

Paul Drewitt doesn't write polite fiction. He punches it in the face and throws it overboard. Known for his raw, unfiltered voice and twisted sense of humor, Drewitt crafts characters you'd cross the street to avoid—but secretly want to follow.

Raised somewhere between a concrete jungle and a moral grey zone, his storytelling draws from real-world absurdity, late-night encounters, and the kind of people you never invite to dinner but always remember. Vince

Lombardi is his unapologetic pushback against sanitized storytelling and the overly polished narratives of modern fiction. He writes because therapy is expensive, and someone has to say what everyone else is thinking.

www.ingramcontent.com/pod-product-compliance
Lightning Source LLC
Chambersburg PA
CBHW070556300726
48975CB00006B/1605